A
KALEIDOSCOPE
of Short Stories

A work of fiction by
F. E. Cassidy

Library of Congress Number: 99-95453
ISBN#0-88100-112-0
in conjunction with national writers press

The stories in this book are a work of fiction. Except for some details associated with the author's life, all incidents and characters relating to the stories are imaginary.

To Margaret,
for patiently listening to these stories--
over and over again.

Kaleidoscope

Short Stories
And Some Very Short Stories

Contents

Acknowledgements

The author wishes to thank the many people in the Fraser Valley and beyond who have offered encouragement, as well as criticism, by reading and reviewing these short stories. I especially thank the members of the Creative Writing Group, Fraser Valley Library (Mary Ann Wilcox, Librarian).

Special thanks are due to Lynne Beykirch for her patient and professional proofreading and editing.

On the Road to Devil's Thumb

As you drive down Colorado State Highway 40, about three miles past Fraser toward Tabernash, look to the right, and you will see a saddle on the farthest ridge. That is the Continental Divide. Halfway up the saddle is a distinct rock protrusion called Devil's Thumb. Actually, it is the very top of a mountain peak jutting up on the east side of the Continental Divide. It is hidden from view on the west side, except for the top of the peak. County Road 83 starts at the Sunset Ridge pond just before the railroad overpass outside of Tabernash. Although CR 83 is often referred to as Devil's Thumb Road, it dead ends at Devil's Thumb Ranch, a few miles up the road.

Irene Roberts made a habit of jogging along Devil's Thumb Road, especially on weekends. She enjoyed the peacefulness, the beautiful snow-capped mountains, and seeing an occasional fox or coyote leaping on mice in the hay meadows along the road. Midsummer in the Fraser Valley, a jogger can usually count on rainy weekends, and this Saturday was no exception. Irene was often heard complaining that it never failed to rain on her days off.

She didn't enjoy running in the rain but wouldn't allow a

Saturday off without getting in at least a few miles. She had delayed as long as she could, and the rain persisted. Normally, she would be finished and out of the shower by nine o'clock. Hoping the rain would let up, she wasted the morning away.

By one o'clock, she decided to get wet, put on her slick waterproof jogging pants, shouted to her two cats she would be right back, opened the door, and plunged into the downpour. Twenty minutes later she was a couple of miles along Devil's Thumb Road and decided the rain was too tough to endure any longer. She would turn back but first wanted to check on the bluebird box at the crest of the steepest part of the road. She had seen bluebirds flying in and out of the nest on recent runs. The box was nailed to a fence post and had been regularly inhabited over the years.

Irene welcomed the rest stop. She usually walked up the steep incline and gasped for breath in the rare air at the 8,800-foot elevation. As she walked close to the box on the post perched precariously on the cliff's edge, she ignored warnings from two bluebirds flying about the bird box. She noticed movement near the base of the fence post. It was a baby bluebird. Too early out of the nest. She knew better than to pick up a grounded bird near a nest but couldn't resist. The young bird was dangerously close to a steep bank which ended at a cliff face 10 or 15 feet down a slope steeper than the roof of a mountain "A" frame.

Irene feared the young bluebird would tumble down the slope, over the cliff, and into Hurd Creek more than 200 feet below. She bent down carefully, ignoring the muddy ground; got on her stomach; and cautiously reached out for the baby bird. She believed she could easily pick up the helpless bird and rescue it from certain death. Suddenly, the bird escaped from her grasp, slid down the slope a few feet, flapped its wings, flew clear of the cliff over the valley, and circled back into the trees. Irene smiled at the episode and turned on her side to crawl back up to safe and level ground. She instantly realized her mistake. The rain made the clay earth slippery and unstable on the slope. She reached out and grabbed a small sapling for support. The rain had soaked deep into the roots. The sapling came out of the rain-soaked soil. She reached for another to stop her slide. It, too, pulled easily out of the ground. She began to slide faster. Her slick, waterproof jogging pants acted like a snowboard on snow. She slid faster and faster toward the cliff's edge. Panic caused her to flail her arms and move her feet as though she was swimming. She knew in an instant she would be dropping feet first off the edge.

Suddenly, she was jarred to a stop, straddling a dead lodge pole pine with one leg on each side of the dead tree. She took a deep breath and regained reasoning. She knew she was saved by the dead tree but for how long? She felt the long-dead pine move slightly from the weight of her body. Somehow, she had to get her footing and crawl back up the slope before the tree moved anymore. Each effort caused the tree to shake and shudder. Panic again took control of her efforts as she visualized both she and the dead tree going over the cliff's edge and being splintered to pieces on the rocks of Hurd Creek below. The slightest motion caused rocks and mud to rattle a short distance away and soundlessly fall into space; there was a muffled thud moments later as they landed in the creek. She thought, "I can't make another move. What can I do?"

Chuck and Chris Cooley walked their black Lab along Devil's Thumb Road most afternoons--usually between three and four o'clock–rain, shine, or snow. They began their trek from a condo at Junction Ranch. The Lab was named Mr. Gander, reflecting imagined origins in Labrador.

Mr. Gander ran freely ahead of the Cooleys across the hay

meadow to County Road 83, darting in all directions to frighten ravens and blackbirds groundfeeding on insects. The dog was careful not to stray too far from the usual path the Cooleys took to the crest above Hurd Creek. The constant rain and drizzle persisted. Chuck hurried his pace, turned, and shouted to Chris, "I'm going to try and get Gander before he gets to the road!"

"O.K.!" Chris called back. "Let's go home anyway. I'm getting wet feet, and it's turning cold. I'm going back. See you at the condo."

"Gander! Here, Gander! Come, Gander, come!" Chuck cupped his hand and called again as loud as he could between shrill whistles. The black Lab was out of sight and into the trees at the left side of the road beyond the crest.

Irene was shivering in the cold, crying and making an effort to fight off frequent spells of sheer panic. She would shout for help but heard only her echo. Her throat was becoming sore from the screams. She thought she had been held by the dead tree for at least three hours, maybe even four. She didn't dare try to look at her watch. To do so, she would need to lift her left arm and was sure that would cause more instability and the tree to move even more. She kept her fingers dug into the soft, wet soil.

Suddenly, her state of panic was interrupted by a barking dog. Carefully, she lifted her head to look up the steep slope and could see the dog 20 or 30 feet up at the crest. "Thank God! There must be someone walking their dog!"

"Help! Somebody, help me. Please!" She shouted as loud as she could; but shaking with the cold, she knew it was not very loud. "Help! Somebody, please help! I'm going to fall over the edge!" There was no response--only the barking dog and the sound of rocks falling to the creek below.

Chuck shouted and whistled continuously. He heard the dog's incessant barking. "Bloody dog has a porcupine treed," he said aloud to himself. "Here Gander; here Gander!"

Irene continued to shout for help, sobbing and crying between frantic calls. The only answer from above was barking echoing through the valley. She watched the dog turn and disappear from sight, still barking. "Please, oh please, don't leave me," she cried.

Chuck saw the Lab finally heeding his call. Moments later the Lab was at his side and barking excitedly. Chuck bent over to calm the dog and at the same time clicked the hasp of his lead strap onto the collar ring. Gander strained to get away. He said to the dog, "Remember the last time you tangled with a porcupine, Gander? You should. You spent a painful time at Byers Peak Veterinary Clinic getting quills pulled out of your nose. We're going home. You'll thank me in the morning." Gander continued to struggle against the lead, but Chuck was determined the dog would get home without porcupine quills sticking out of his snout. As they approached the condo, Gander quieted down and seemed to have forgotten the attraction back at the crest over Hurd Creek. Before opening the condo door, Chuck bent over to remove the lead. As Gander felt the slack, he quickly pulled away and ran back toward the hay meadow and the hill crest two miles away, dragging the lead behind.

Chuck started running after the dog but thought better and, hurried back to the condo, opened the door, and shouted, "Chris, come quickly, bring the car keys! Gander has taken off for Devil's Thumb Road. We'll have to put him in the car to bring him back." Chris threw a rain cape over her shoulders and came running to the door holding out the car keys.

"O.K., let's go! You drive so I can jump out as soon as we see him." Chuck opened the passenger's side door and hurriedly got in.

In the car Chuck said with a worried tone, "I think we may be taking him to the vet if he tangles with another porcupine. I don't understand. Gander has always obeyed commands. Something's gotten into him. I've never seen him act this way."

As they turned at Devil's Thumb junction and sped up the road, Chris pointed toward the top of the hill beyond the hay meadow. "I think I see him. He's headed toward the wooded area at the crest." Chuck had his hand on the door handle ready to jump out as soon as the car stopped.

Irene was feeling cold and was shaking. Rain was still falling, and a breeze drifted up from the valley floor intensifying the chill. She couldn't stop sobbing, almost reconciled to the thought that no one would come to rescue her. She was doomed to fall over the edge to death below. The dead tree was moving slowly with her weight. Both feet were over the cliff's edge; there was nothing solid she could feel to support herself. Hysteria and hypothermia mixed, causing random, nonsensical illusions. With a short, hysterical laugh, she thought of a strip in the *Denver Post* comic section which often depicted Sergeant Snorkel hanging from a branch on a cliff face while Private Beetle Bailey stood by wondering what to do. She had no Beetle Bailey standing by. She thought of her Creative Writing Group, which met weekly at the Fraser Valley Library, and how she could write a real "cliff hanger" story. Again, she gave a soft, hysterical giggle and said aloud, "I don't like the ending."

A barking dog brought her back to reality and her precarious plight. She again cautiously looked up the steep, muddy slope. It was the same black dog which had been there a half hour or so earlier.

"Help!" she shouted with a half hope that maybe

someone would be with the dog.

Chuck heard a muffled cry as he approached Gander, who was running excitedly along the top of the slope. He called out, "Hello! Is someone down there?"

"Yes! Please help me. I'm about to fall off the cliff. Help me!"

"O.K., lady. Hang on. I'll get you up." Chuck eased toward the slope's edge and could clearly see Irene's precarious position. "Hang on, I'll try to get down to you."

"No! For God's sake! Don't try to come down the slope. It's very slippery. You might slide all the way; we'll both go over! This tree is moving; it won't support both of us."

Chuck could hear Irene's voice crack with panic. "All right, I'll get help. Stay where you are; I"ll be back in a minute."

"Stay where you are!" Irene said out loud. "Where does he think I'm going?"

Chuck ran to the car with Mr. Gander running alongside with his lead trailing. "Chris! There's a girl hanging on the cliff about to go over! Quickly, drive up the road and get to a phone; call 9-1-1 for help. Hurry, I think she is about to fall. That's why Gander was barking. He found her." Chuck ran back up to the slope's edge, Gander at his side.

He could hear Irene gasping, "Help! Help!" Chuck cupped his hands and called down the slope. "Calm down, help is coming." He could hear spasmodic sobs.

In an effort to relax her, Chuck calmly called out, "What's your name?"

"Irene Roberts," was a hoarse reply. "I live in Tabernash. If I fall, please see that my two cats are taken care of. They're alone in the house."

"Now don't worry; you'll be taking care of them yourself." Chuck inched closer to the slope's edge, holding onto an anchored lodge pole pine. "My name is Chuck Cooley. My wife, Chris, has gone to find a phone to call 9-1-1."

Irene hesitated a moment and replied, "Chris Cooley, I know her. She works at the resort."

"Yes, she works at the resort. She'll get help. Just try and relax; you'll be O.K."

Chris stopped at two homes along the road. Both were locked. No one answered her knocks and calls. The third stop was The Claddagh B&B off Devil's Thumb Road. She dialed 9-1-1 and set the rescue in motion.

The emergency call was relayed from the Colorado State Patrol dispatcher at the Hot Sulphur Springs Sheriff's office to the East Grand Fire Station between Winter Park and Fraser. Individual pagers sounded along the valley, summoning volunteers from restaurants, motel desks, house building sites, tee shirt shops, and the hardware store. Within minutes Rescue/Pumper 482, Ambulance 221, and a Search & Rescue vehicle were speeding through Fraser, heading down Highway 40 toward Devil's Thumb Road.

Chris had joined Chuck on the muddy slope's crest. "Search and Rescue is on the way, Chuck." She took the still-attached lead from Mr. Gander's collar. Chuck told her it was Irene Roberts hanging on the edge of the cliff. Chris called, "Help is on the way, Irene. I can see the emergency lights coming down Highway 40. They should be here in a couple of minutes."

Search and Rescue pulled up near Chris' parked car, followed by the rescue/pumper. Three rescue volunteers hurried to the crest of the slope. The mission leader quietly gave instructions to the two other volunteers. Chuck and Chris, Mr. Gander, and the B&B owner stood back to watch the rescue teams go into action. Within minutes, there were ropes, pulleys, a Stokes litter, and the rescue team in body harnesses moving methodically over the slope. On Hurd Creek Road, a second rescue team was moving towards a point directly below Irene preparing to climb up the cliff from the creek, if need be.

Minutes later, Irene was strapped in the Stokes litter and pulled up on ropes anchored to the rescue/pumper. A moment later, Chris was comforting Irene as she was lifted to the ambulance and quickly en route to the Granby Medical Clinic 15 miles away.

Irene became a local celebrity but was always embarrassed to talk about her terrible ordeal. The event was described on the front page of the local newspaper, the *Winter Park Manifest*, complete with a photograph of the sheer cliff along Hurd Creek. A graphic arrow pointed to the spot where she had spent those terrifying hours.

Weeks later, Irene was back into her jogging routine. She approached the blue bird box on Devil's Thumb road and couldn't resist the temptation to peer over the slope, holding on tightly to a fence post. She could see her saving tree was still there but leaning a bit more over the cliff than when she last saw it. Suddenly, she felt a gentle tug on her right pant leg. Startled, she carefully backed away from the fence post to level ground and turned to see Mr. Gander. She imagined he was smiling as he turned from her and ran toward Chuck Cooley's whistle from a distance down in the hay meadow.

Kaleidoscope

Nevermore

On a sunny day in April a few years ago, I was sitting on the deck at our home in the mountains, enjoying the warmth of the spring sun and watching the birds who were also enjoying the sunshine after a long and cold winter. Suddenly, I saw a Brown Tail Hawk swoop from high and strike a raven which had been feeding on table scraps in our bird feeder. The bird tumbled in the air as he fell to the ground, and the hawk flew off to look for other prey.

I slowly walked over to the fallen raven, believing he had been killed by the hawk's terrifying blow. To my surprise, the bird was alive but badly injured. His left wing was stretched out without movement. The raven was very weak from the blow. I picked him up; he didn't seem to struggle to get free of my grip. I took the bird into our garden room and constantly rubbed his head. I had heard that rubbing a bird's head after an injury, such as flying into a window, could help it revive.

I kept the injured raven in our garden room for the next month, feeding him pieces of meat and other scraps of food which he seemed to enjoy and ate readily. We became such friends I gave the bird a name, Nevermore, after the raven in the Edgar Allen Poe poem. I continued to rub Nevermore's head often during his recovery. He seemed to expect the attention.

His injuries improved greatly. He would limp in short hops around the garden room and look out the windows longing to be outside once again and flying free.

I decided it was time for Nevermore to return to the wilds. He seemed to be healed well enough to care for himself. While the raven perched on my hand having his head stroked for the last time, I opened the door to release him. He quickly flew off to the nearest tree branch and perched. Shortly after, he flew across the meadow and out of sight into the forest.

Later that summer, I was hiking alone on a remote mountain trail. It had been a wet summer, and there was moss growing on rocks in the shaded areas along the trail. The trail became steeper; the rocks were very slippery and made it difficult for me to get a safe footing. Suddenly, I felt my right foot slipping away. There was nothing close enough for me to grab to steady myself. My walking stick was no help. I slid down a steep slope, my head struck a tree trunk, and I saw stars and lost consciousness.

My next recollection was like waking from a dream. I could only hear a loud "kaw, kaw" very close to my head. I opened my eyes; and not more than a few feet away, perched on a rock, was a lone raven. He was calling continuously while looking straight into my eyes. I was still stunned and did not move. The raven continued uninterrupted calling loudly, "Kaw, kaw!" He hopped to my left boot and perched on the toe, still calling anxiously, as if to say, "Get up, get up!"

Slowly, I sat up. The raven stayed close to me. He had stopped calling. After regaining my senses, I stood up and held my aching head with both hands. The raven quietly hopped closer and continued looking directly at me. I picked up my walking stick, struggled back to the trail, and headed home. It took an hour to negotiate my way down the trail. The raven never left my side, always flying to within a few feet and occasionally calling, "Kaw, kaw", as if to say, "Keep going; you are doing fine!"

As I reached our home, close to the back door, I stopped and faced the raven. He hopped away with a slight limp and flew off into the forest. It was then that I knew, the raven was Nevermore.

Editor's Note:

"Nevermore" first appeared in the December 23, 1998, issue of the Winter Park Manifest. *The reviewer noted: "While (Fran) has indeed, nursed a few birds in his garden room and returned them to the wild, the reader can only guess where truth and fiction merge in this short story titled 'Nevermore'."*

Ben Dog

Albert sat in his favorite living-room chair opposite the 19-inch television which sat on an "end table" more resembling a box than a piece of furniture. His television provided many, many hours of entertainment from sports broadcasts to old-time movies and always the news at 6:00 p.m.

At thirty years, his life had few memorable events; but he was generally happy with his daily routine. He was up at 7:00 every weekday and at his desk and computer at World Freight, Inc., by 8:30. He liked his job, routing unseen packages to faraway places. If he had designed a long-term plan for his future, he would have included visits to places unfamiliar to his friends in countries they couldn't spell. But his plan for the future seldom included anything that could not be accomplished in a month's time. He played golf at the local municipal course every Saturday morning with his regular foursome and went to church on Sunday morning, provided he didn't sleep in after a long night at Flynn's neighborhood tavern.

All in all, his life was comfortable, uneventful, and without a lot of responsibility. On this Friday evening, he sat half reading the morning paper and half listening to the day's news, which was mostly local issues, such as parents' battles with a local school board, a house fire on 8th Street, pending local election issues, and traffic lights out on Main. The same news in the same words were also in the local paper, *The Daily Dispatch*, the only paper Eagle Grove had, not that there was need for more. In fact, the paper struggled to generate enough news stories to fill the half dozen pages which sandwiched news articles between ads for used cars, grocery store specials, and bargains at the local Gambels store. Political ads also took up a lot of space at the time of the various, frequent elections in town. Generally, the *Dispatch* satisfied the 7,000-some souls who lived in Eagle Grove and on the surrounding farms.

On this particular Friday evening, Albert's life was to experience a change, a change for which he would never plan nor believe would ever occur. But then, he seldom considered any change to his daily, weekly, or monthly routines.

The front doorbell rang. It was strange for anyone to come by on a Friday evening. In all likelihood, someone was selling something or soliciting a donation for a cause in which he had no interest. Without turning down the sound on the TV, he got up from his chair and went to open the front door. Still holding the *Dispatch*, Albert opened the door; and within a second or two, he recognized Kurt Beck, his one-time roommate in junior college.

"Kurt!?" He greeted Kurt with more question in his voice than welcome. He shook Kurt's extended hand. "What brings you here? How did you find me? Come on in."

Kurt readily accepted the invitation and followed Albert into the living room. Albert went and turned off the TV. Kurt filled the sudden silence. "Al, it is really good to see you after all these years. How long has it been? Ten or eleven years? You haven't changed. It looks like you're doing well. These are nice digs--lots better than our rooms at old Mrs. Moses, eh?" Kurt laughed. Albert nodded agreement with a slight grin, remembering the spartan and cluttered rooms they shared at Mrs. Moses' boarding house.

"What are you up to, Kurt? What have you been doing? Where are you living?" Albert tried to sound sincere, knowing as he said the words that he really wasn't interested in answers-- whatever they might be.

"Oh, I've been traveling quite a bit, so I can't really say where I live. Mostly, I've been doing odd jobs as a carpenter's helper, hanging sheetrock, and painting some houses. I even had my own business for awhile with the house painting. I called myself 'The Painter Man' but gave that up. Couldn't pay the bills. I knew you came from Eagle Grove; and when I saw the exit sign on the interstate, I thought I would take a chance and try to find you; and here I am. I found you."

Albert was feeling a little apprehensive, not knowing what Kurt's intents might be or how they would involve him. From their short time together, he remembered Kurt as a not-very-reliable guy, who was often called "The Sponge" by their classmates. Kurt appeared to be reasonably dressed and clean, so Albert thought that he probably wouldn't be hitting him up for a 'loan'. Maybe, at the most, he was looking for a place to spend the night."

"How about a beer, Kurt? I was just about to open one myself. What do you say?" Albert got out of his chair and headed for the kitchen before Kurt could answer.

"Sure, I'd like a beer. I'm not going to stay long. I just wanted to take the opportunity to see you again, Al." Kurt spoke loud enough to be heard in the kitchen. Albert breathed a quiet sigh, relieved to hear that his uninvited guest was not likely to be a big problem for him.

He took two bottles of Grain Belt to the living room and handed one to Kurt, and asked, "Do you still drink from the bottle or do you want a glass?"

Kurt took the bottle and replied, "No glass; I still drink from the bottle. Beer loses something when you pour it into a glass." He took a sip from the bottle and put it on a side table. "Al, I've got my dog in the van. Do you mind if I bring him in? He's been cooped up for hours. He won't be any trouble. He's very well behaved." Kurt got up from his chair and headed for the front door, believing Albert would not object.

"Sure, Kurt, bring him in. There's nothing in here he could hurt." Albert knew he couldn't refuse and really didn't mind a dog in the house. He liked animals but would never think of having one. They were too restricting.

Kurt brought the dog into the house. "Here is Ben Dog; he's been my pal for quite a few years." Ben Dog appeared to be a mixture of collie, retriever, and maybe something else. He seemed to be friendly and took to Albert as if looking for acceptance, as well as a scratch behind his floppy ears.

As Albert petted Ben Dog, Kurt said, "Al, you won't believe what I came across in some boxes I've had since we were in school. An album of pictures. Would you like to see them? Lots of them are of us doing stupid stunts. I'll go get them if you like."

"Sure, bring them in. I'm not all that sure I really want to see them. We did a lot of silly things back then that I really would like to forget," Albert said with a laugh.

Kurt was gone a long time. More than fifteen minutes passed, and Albert wondered how much junk Kurt had to go through to find the album. He looked at the bottle Kurt had hardly touched and thought the beer would be warm by now. He got up and went to the window to see if he could tell why Kurt was taking so long. Ben Dog had settled down into a comfortable spot on the carpet as though he belonged there and took no notice of Albert's movements.

Albert was astonished as he looked out the window and saw nothing of Kurt--no van, nothing. He went to the front door and looked up and down the street--no Kurt, no van, nobody! He stood dumfounded for several minutes. The realization came to him with a shock. He had just inherited Ben Dog!

A Dog's Prayer Answered

George Cupps sat at the kitchen table with a semi-warm mug of coffee. Lately, at 8:30 on most mornings, George could be found in the same spot thinking the same thoughts. He held a short pencil above a ruled pad of paper that had scattered, penciled figures put there that morning and the morning before and even from the morning before that. They all seemed to come to the same numerical conclusion. George was close to flat broke, out of money. The small pension check from the hardware store combined with a social security check simply did not total enough to maintain his lifestyle, spartan as it was.

In the days before he canceled his morning paper subscription, he had often read that the government was proud that inflation was under control. This was more than a little confusing to George since nearly everyday he could see prices of everything going up. Certainly, nothing was cheaper than a year ago, and most things cost more.

He was no economist, but it didn't take much addition or subtraction for him to realize he could no longer afford to keep his car. It had to be sold not just for the cash it would bring but because of the realization that he could no longer afford to pay for the insurance, license, or even the gas to run it. It wasn't that he couldn't make do without the car, but the consequences of being without it bothered him. It bothered him for one reason, a reason most people would call ridiculous. That reason was Nellie.

Nellie sat close to George as she did every morning and most of the day and all of the night. She was not a purebred Golden Retriever but close enough to have all the best traits of a retriever and maybe some better ones that only a mongrel would have.

Nellie was a six-month-old puppy when George's wife Irene had her fatal heart attack twelve years earlier. Since that sad and tragic event, Nellie was George's close companion every hour of the day. No matter where George went, Nellie was with him. She never had to be coaxed into the car and by habit sat in the front seat as a welcomed passenger. She usually had her head stuck out of the window with her ears flapping in the wind when it wasn't raining or too cold to have the window cranked down.

That was the problem that troubled George. By selling the car, he would have to take busses to do his errands; and worse, there would be no more daily trips to the edge of town where Nellie was turned loose to run along the creek and wander through the woods sniffing the special spots which had become so familiar to her over the past twelve years. This had become a happy, daily ritual for both of them.

George didn't like the idea of leaving Nellie alone in the house while he went about his errands. As he turned and faced Nellie, she looked at him as though she could read his thoughts and was pleading with her eyes, "Please don't get rid of the car." He knew he had no choice. He simply couldn't afford not to. It had to be done that very day.

The decision was made. It had become difficult trying to

hide the seeds of poverty. He kept a neat and tidy appearance, shaved and clean. Although a jacket or sweater would show wear at the elbows, most people would believe it was simply a favorite and he couldn't part with it.

George picked up the car title and keys from the counter, put on his cap, and slowly walked to the door which opened into the garage. It seemed as though Nellie hesitated a moment but then moved quickly to join George on his drive wherever it would take them. He bent down to scratch behind her shaggy ears.

"Sorry, old girl; I can't take you with me this time. I'm afraid I will be coming back on the bus, and they just won't allow dogs on a bus no matter how well they behave. I won't be long. We'll take a walk when I get back." As he spoke, he knew Nellie would not be pleased walking on a leash and only around the block; but that is what the future would dictate.

She looked at him with disbelief. Whenever George went to the car, she always went with him without fail. "How could this be happening?" Her eyes asked the question. Nevertheless, she understood she was not to go. She lay down on the kitchen floor with a hope he would change his mind, open the door, and call her. Then she heard the garage door open, the car start, and knew that it wasn't going to happen. She put her nose close to the door and would stay that way until he came back regardless of how long it might be.

George drove slowly down the street on his way to the Empire Used Car Lot. At least he knew that Duke Pritchard would give him the best price he could. He and Duke had been friends for many years, and their wives had been the closest of friends. With both their wives gone, Duke and George became even closer in their mutual sorrow.

When George drove into the car lot, Duke appeared from nowhere with a friendly greeting. "Have you really decided to sell the car, George?" Duke asked with more concern in his voice than question.

"Yes, Duke. I figured every way I can, and just don't see how I can afford to keep it. I know it will be hard to manage without, but it would be a lot harder if I kept it."

George opened the door and handed Duke the car title. "Do the best you can for me, Duke; but I don't want you to lose money on the deal. It is still a good car. I have taken care of it, and it looks pretty good even if it is 14 years old. You know, I put new tires on it only last year, so they don't have many miles on them--maybe only six or seven thousand."

George looked at the ground, trying to keep Duke from seeing the emotion of his disappointment. He then looked toward the trailer that served as Duke's office and softly said, "You know the biggest reason I hate to give the car up is Nellie. I know that sounds ridiculous, but I don't go anywhere without that dog. I will miss not being able to take her with me." George took a deep breath, trying to contain his composure. He wasn't sure how Duke would feel about his concern.

"Yes, I know how close you are to your dog, George. You needn't explain. In fact, it will look odd to see you without Nellie; I don't think I have ever seen you out and about without her." Duke put his hand gently on George's shoulder and said, "Let's go inside and see what we can do."

George walked out of the used car lot and turned up the street toward the bus stop a half block away. He looked at the check Duke had given him and was sure it was much more than the car was worth. When Duke told him how much he would pay for the car, George objected and said it was too much. Duke had said, "Hey, George, I'm the car dealer. I ought to know what a car is worth. You have taken excellent care of that car, and it won't be on the lot more than a few days. Somebody will drive it out of here knowing they bought a very clean car. Don't worry about it. Take the check to the bank while I still have the money to back it up!" They both had laughed at the remark. George knew that Duke could never bring himself to write a bad check. Duke had said, "Come on, I'll give you a ride to the bank and then home."

George had answered: "Thanks, Duke, but I might just as well get used to taking the bus. Besides, you are here alone, and there might be a big customer come while you are gone. I'll be O.K. Thanks again."

George was gone nearly two hours. Taking a bus to the bank and then waiting again for a bus was not very satisfying, especially with having to transfer to get another bus to take him to a stop closer to home. The whole procedure was strange. He had very little experience with public transportation of any sort.

He opened the front door, and Nellie was there to greet him. All her disappointment and the interminable wait were forgotten the second she heard his footsteps on the front porch. George gave Nellie a pet and walked to the kitchen table. He looked at the figures he had written on the pad earlier, shook his head, and thought even selling the car would not help very much. His IRA was just about used up, his small savings account was now so small he wondered if it was worth trying to keep, and the bank loan was still outstanding. Despair was beginning to get a toehold.

Two months went by. Things had not improved. George thought he literally had to count pennies. It didn't help to see the deterioration in Nellie. She was no longer playful. She hated the short walks on a leash around the block to the extent that George had to coax her to go. She was also showing flab from lack of exercise and was listless, sleeping most of the day. This was not unlike the attitude George, himself, developed.

He was sitting, as usual, at the kitchen table when he heard the mail being delivered to the mailbox on his front porch. He didn't move for some time. Lately, he hated to get mail out of fear there would be bills he finally couldn't pay. With lethargy, he got up from the table, walked around Nellie who showed no interest, went to the front door, picked the mail from the box, and with resignation went back to his chair at the kitchen table.

It looked as though there were no bills. For that, he was thankful. There were just some glossy catalogs which went straight into the wastebasket under the sink. He didn't bother to open them, because there was no chance he could afford anything out of them. But there was one letter of interest; he studied the handwriting which was very neat and clear. He looked at the stamp. It was from Eire. The return address read, "Kylemore Abbey, Letterfrack, County Connemara, Eire." He took a pocketknife from his pants pocket and carefully slid the blade under the envelope flap. There were two pages with the same, clear handwriting and another sealed envelope which he put aside. He read the date and the return address which were repeated in the upper right corner of the first page. The letter read:

Dear Mr. Cupps,

I am writing to you concerning a most urgent matter. I am Sister Mary Theresa of the Benedictine Order. I don't know if you have ever had an occasion to know of me; however, I must tell you that we are distant cousins on your mother's side. Your mother was Mary Murphy, whose parents were both born in County Cork, married in Blarney, and shortly after emigrated to America.

I will not go into the details in this letter; however, a careful and thorough investigation was made by Mr. Patrick O'Brien, who is a very reputable solicitor in Dublin. He has confirmed our relationship and has the legal documents to prove the claim.

I have included an envelope in this letter. You will find a prepaid, round-trip, airline ticket to Shannon. There are also confirmation documents for a prepaid rental car to be picked up at the Shannon Airport upon your arrival. Please forgive me for my presumptuousness, but I have had to confirm dates for your visit, providing, of course, that you agree to come. I believe I have allowed sufficient time for you to obtain the necessary travel documents, such as a passport, if you do not already have one. If you find the dates are not suitable for your travel, please contact Mr. O'Brien as soon as possible. His telephone number is included in the separate envelope. You will also find a U.S. dollar cashier's check for $1,000. I trust this will take care of any expenses you might incur in preparing for your trip. Please use this money as you see fit. There is no need to maintain a record of expenditure. Also included is a map marked with the route to the Abbey. I have booked you in the Flynn Bed and Breakfast in the village of Letterfrack for the dates as shown.

As you can see, I feel it is of utmost importance for both of us that you come to Ireland as requested. I will be forever in your debt if you will do so. I do apologize for not providing more details of this urgent cause for your visit. This is due to the advice of Mr. O'Brien. All will be clear upon your arrival.

I am most certainly looking forward to meeting you.

Respectfully, I am,

Sister Mary Theresa (Murphy)
Benedictine Order

George opened the separate envelope he had put aside. The airline ticket and other documents were there, as described. He sat in wonder for several minutes. "What in the world is this all about? I have to talk to Duke. Maybe he will have some thoughts about it and can advise me."

George took the envelopes and put them in his jacket pocket. He walked to the front door and Nellie only looked at him not making a move to go with him. That was usual of late. Nellie had lost interest in George's movements.

He walked to the bus stop and stood for 15 minutes until the bus finally came along. In another 30 minutes, he was at the Empire Used Car Lot.

"Duke, will you read this letter and tell me what you think?" He sat across the cluttered desk from Duke.

Duke took the envelopes and began reading the letter. He then looked at the tickets and other documents and the $1,000 check.

He gave a low whistle and said, "Your cousin must really want to see you!" He looked at George with a slight frown on his face. "I see no reason why you shouldn't take the trip. See what it is all about. You have nothing to lose and maybe something to gain."

"Yes, I suppose you're right. What about Nellie? I don't think I can leave her. She doesn't seem too well lately, and I won't put her in a kennel; that would kill her. I will be gone nearly a week. I could use some of the $1,000 to pay to board her, but I just won't do that--not for anything or anybody." George looked out of the trailer window but really was seeing nothing, deep in thought.

Duke stroked his chin and quietly said: "Do it George. I can take care of Nellie. She can lay around here in the office just as well as at your house, and I will take her home with me in the evening. Go ahead and take them up on their offer. If nothing else, you will have an opportunity to see Ireland. Go ahead and do it."

George remained quiet, staring out of the trailer window. After a couple of minutes, he faced Duke. "O.K., I'll do it. It is very kind of you to offer to take care of the dog. Thanks. I'll repay you somehow."

"Don't think about repaying me. There is nothing to repay. I'm happy to do it. Now go to the Post Office and apply for a passport," Duke said.

"No, I don't have to. Remember when Irene and I took that trip to Costa Rica with the church group? We got passports at that time, and I have kept mine renewed for some reason. It is still valid."

"Great," Duke said. "Then take some of that $1,000 and buy a new suit and shoes, the works. Your cousin said spend it for whatever is necessary for your trip, and that is necessary for your trip." As an afterthought, Duke added "For sure!"

"Duke, since I have some money to spend, would you call a taxi for me? I'll go to the bank and cash this check and then I will look for some new clothes." George smiled with comfort that he was doing the right thing. In fact, he felt a bit of a boost at the thought of taking a trip to Ireland regardless of the cause.

A few weeks later, George was on his way to Ireland and an adventure of which he couldn't have dreamed a month before. He landed in Shannon on schedule, but he felt very strange. It was his first experience with jet lag. He asked directions to the car rental counter three times. He could not understand the Irish brogue the first two times. After getting directions to Letterfrack from the rental car attendant, he was in the car and on his way but very slowly, much to the annoyance and occasional horn blast from people in cars following him. He was trying not to be fearful of driving on the left side of the road with the steering wheel on the right side of the car. It was all very strange to George.

Out of Shannon and on the route outlined on the map, he began to build confidence and actually started to notice the scenery instead of the car directly ahead. Hours later, he approached the Kylemore Abbey. He was struck with its beauty. In his entire life, he had never seen a place quite like it. The abbey was much like a castle nestled in a very green, heavily forested valley with steep hills on both sides. The hills gradually lost trees as he looked to the hilltops. He guessed that what he was seeing was heather on the hilltops.

He parked the car which was unscathed in spite of numerous close shaves on the narrow Irish road. The walk up to the turreted castle wound by ancient oak trees and tall conifers that were so full that sunlight did not penetrate to the walkway.

George entered the abbey through huge oak doors which

were ornately carved. Inside, there was a slight smell of oak wood smoke; it was more like incense mixed with a pleasant scent of antique furniture, fixtures, and polished wood. He noticed that the door casings looked like works of art, polished smooth with the grain showing through. He walked across the lobby to a reception desk. There was no one in sight. A small brass bell sat on top of a handwritten note which read, "Please ring for attendant." He shook the bell once and quickly put it back in place, a little embarrassed with the sound. A young-looking nun in habit appeared behind the desk-like counter. "May I help you, sir?" she asked in a soft voice with a strong Irish lilt.

"Yes, thank you. My name is George Cupps. I'm from the United States. Sister Mary Theresa is expecting me." George ended his introduction with his best-formed smile.

"Oh! Yes! Sister Mary Theresa will be very pleased you are here. She is expecting you. Please follow me to the lounge, and I will call her immediately." The young nun lead George into a very comfortable-looking room with a sofa and overstuffed easy chairs covered in rich tapestry. Leather-bound books lined two of the walls.

"Please make yourself comfortable. Sister Theresa will be with you shortly. May I offer you some tea?"

"No thank you," George said as he relaxed in one of the overstuffed chairs. A few minutes passed, and another nun walked into the study. She appeared to be in her late sixties or early seventies, but it was difficult to tell at first glance because her skin looked like that of a much younger person, and her eyes were also bright and young looking. For an instant, George thought he could detect a resemblance in an old photograph of his mother.

"Hello! You must be George Cupps!" Before George could answer, she went on: "I have looked forward to meeting you so much! I am your cousin, Mary Theresa Murphy," she said as she grabbed George's right hand and shook it vigorously.

"Yes, Sister. I am George Cupps, and it is a pleasure to meet you also. I must first thank you for your generosity in sending me a plane ticket and arranging a car and a place to stay. Especially, I want to thank you for sending a thousand dollars! I must confess, I am afraid it would have been impossible for me to come here if you hadn't. I have trouble making ends meet at the present. Thank you. You have been very kind." George became flush; he realized he was talking too fast and too much. He thought, "Maybe it is the jet lag I have heard about."

"George, you are most welcome. It was a pleasure and, more, worth every pound to have you agree to come and to have you here safely." She spoke with much less Irish lilt than the young nun and with a clearly educated and trained voice. "Come, let us take a stroll down the chapel path while I tell you what this mystery is all about."

They walked without speaking through the lobby and through the oaken doors, down the steps, and out onto a path. The chapel could be seen through the oak trees about a hundred yards away. Halfway toward the chapel, she stopped at a garden bench along the path. "Let's sit here while I tell you the story." George nodded approval and sat with Sister Mary Theresa.

"Well, I will begin by telling you that I am the last of the Murphys. My older brother passed on about a year ago, God rest his soul. Our family had a farm holding in County Cork. When my parents died many years ago, my brother continued to work the farm and maintained a flock of sheep." As she said it, three sheep slowly walked in front of them.

George expressed surprise. "Speaking of sheep, do these wander at will on the grounds?"

The nun smiled and said, "Oh, yes. We have many sheep grazing on the property. No one bothers them, and you may notice there are no fences. But, of course, most of the flocks in this part of Ireland roam over great distances where there are no fences. The owners mark their sheep with a dye in order to keep track of them."

She turned and looked directly at George. "To continue, my brother maintained the farm until his death. He had no children to continue the operation. I took a vow of poverty at age twenty when I joined the Benedictine Order, so I have no interest and am unable to attempt to continue the farm operation or to rent or lease the farm. Therefore, I had no choice but to arrange for the farm to be sold. Our family solicitor, Mr. O'Brien, took care of all of the arrangements. By the way, he will meet with us at your B&B tomorrow morning for breakfast about 8:30, if that is acceptable for you?"

George said, "Of course, it is acceptable for me. Please continue."

"A short time ago, the farm was sold. I decided to give half of the proceeds to this abbey and believed the balance should go to you, my only living relative." The nun smiled.

George showed surprise and scratched the back of his neck nervously as he expressed his thanks.

"I am not at all sure what amount of money is involved, but we should hear all about that from Mr. O'Brien tomorrow morning. Now, I know you must be very tired from your plane trip and your drive to get here. I suggest you go to the B&B and rest up. I will explain the best way to get there. I hope you didn't have too many problems driving on the opposite side of the road from what you are used to."

George shrugged his shoulders and said, "No, I didn't have a problem once I got the hang of it. In fact, I surprised myself."

"Very well then; we'll go back to the abbey, and I'll show you the way to Letterfrack."

As they strolled along, George could not get over the beauty of the place. Rhododendrons were in bloom everywhere. Bleeding heart vines covered the ancient walls. It was certainly the most beautiful place he had ever seen. The nun explained that the abbey was build as a castle in the mid 1800s and that the Benedictine Order occupied it in the early 1920s after World War I. This order of Benedictine Trappists were in Belgium although they were first formed in Normandy. Their monastery in Belgium was destroyed in the war, and the order moved to Ireland and made the old castle into a convent school as it is today. Sister Mary Theresa had been a teacher at the convent since joining the order.

George found the Flynn B&B with little problem. He was warmly welcomed and shown to his room. He sat on the bed to think of the revelations and happenings of the day. Within a few minutes, his head was on the pillow, and he was sound asleep, clothes and all.

The next morning, he felt well rested and was in the breakfast room promptly at 8:30. Both, Sister Mary Theresa and Mr. O'Brien, were seated at a breakfast table. O'Brien stood up and took a step toward George, holding out his hand as a warm greeting. "Hello, George. I am Patrick O'Brien. It is a pleasure to meet you. Please sit down."

"Thank you, it is a pleasure to meet you." George faced Sister Theresa and smiled, "Good morning, Sister."

Before he could say anything further, Sister Theresa said, "I hope you slept well; you look rested. Are the accommodations to your liking; I do hope so."

George waved his arm expressing satisfaction. "Everything is really wonderful. I could stay here forever!"

"Mr. Cupps," O'Brien said, "I believe Sister Theresa has explained her intents concerning the proceeds from the sale of the Murphy family farm in County Cork. As you are now aware, you are Sister Theresa's only living relative. I also believe you know that we have made a careful investigation to confirm that. I felt it was necessary for you to come to Ireland in order that we could explain in person the circumstance of the transaction; and, of course, Sister Theresa wished to meet you. Thank you for your cooperation and making the trip over here."

O'Brien went over lengthy, legal details of the entire sales transaction while a very complete Irish breakfast was served by both Mr. and Mrs. Flynn. George was barely listening to O'Brien, wondering why they felt it necessary to include him in such detailed discussions.

O'Brien said, "Mr. Cupps, I am afraid we haven't been able to establish an exact amount of money to be received from the holdings sale at this time and will not be able to until certain debts and tax matters are settled. I apologize; I know you understand these matters take time."

There was a warm parting conversation as they left the breakfast room. George promised to return to Ireland sometime in the future, knowing it was an idle promise. He would never be able to afford it.

Duke was sitting at his desk while George described the Irish adventure in detail. Nellie was at his side showing her obvious joy at having George back again.

"Duke, I don't expect anything to come of this. O'Brien mentioned there were debts and taxes against the Murphy farm sale. I think my airline ticket and the thousand dollars will be the sum total I can expect. I just hope the sale doesn't leave my cousin a lot of debt. Maybe I will have to pay them back so I'm not spending anymore of that thousand dollars except for one more taxi fare. Will you call one? I'm going to take Nellie home. Thanks for taking care of her. I hope she wasn't any trouble. I'll pay you back somehow."

Duke picked up the phone to call a taxi and said, "Forget it, George; I was happy to do it. She was no trouble at all."

George was back at the same old spot at the kitchen table with stained coffee mug at hand when the phone rang. This was a rare event.

"Hello, George? This is Ted Brown." Ted was the manager of the Valley Bank, which held his outstanding loan.

George's heart sank. Ted sounded very serious, and George knew that could mean no good. "Yes, Ted, what can I do for you?"

"George, would you please come down to the bank now?"

This was it! The bank was calling in his loan. He couldn't pay it. Impossible. The loan stood at over $5,000 plus interest.

"Sure, Ted I can get down there now, but it will take a little while. I sold my car so I have to take the bus."

"No George, I'll send my secretary to pick you up. She will leave right away. See you shortly. Good-bye, George." Ted hung up.

George held his head in both hands. Nellie came close, sensing that something was not right.

"Nellie, I'm going down to the bank. When I get back, we may not have a home. That's called homeless for both of us." He gently patted Nellie.

Ted had a very somber look, which was uncharacteristic–at least in past meetings George had had with him.

"George, I'll get right to the heart of the matter."

"Here it comes," thought George.

"Are you familiar with a Mr. Patrick O'Brien, a lawyer in Dublin, Ireland?"

"Yes, I know Mr. O'Brien. We actually met last week in Ireland. I have a cousin there who paid my way over. O'Brien is her attorney handling the sale of the family farm. What does he want?" George had a deep-furrowed frown.

"Mr. O'Brien has made a bank transfer to your account on behalf of a Sister Mary Theresa--Murphy in the amount of six hundred fifty-eight thousand two hundred thirty-eight dollars and twelve cents!" Brown's eyes widened to two bright moons with a full-faced smile.

George stared at Ted Brown. "Don't kid me, Ted. It's a joke, isn't it?

"No, George. Here, see for yourself." Ted passed the documents across the desk to George. "It's all legal, and the money, all of it, is yours!"

George walked out of the bank in a daze. He had signed the papers, and his bank account was bulging with over a half million dollars! He had Brown call a taxi, which was waiting at curbside. He gave directions to the driver to take him to the Empire Used Car Lot.

"Duke, I just got some money from that cousin in Ireland, and I want to buy a car!"

"Sure, George. Hey, I still have your car on the lot. I'll sell it back to you for what I paid you for it. How's that?" Duke gave George a big smile.

"Yeah, you told me my car wouldn't be on the lot for more than a few days, and you still have it. I don't want that heap. I want a new car! How about that baby over there?" George pointed at a new black Lincoln Town Car that almost looked like a limousine.

"Oh, George, that car is listed for over $40,000. It would take you forever to pay if off. Don't spend all your Irish money on a car. I can put you into a very nice, clean, used car that will do you just fine. Come on; let's look around."

"No Duke, I will pay you cash for that Lincoln now. In fact, I won't give you less than $50,000, and that is my firm and final offer. Let's go get the title. And by the way, look for a new Airstream trailer for me. Nellie and I are going to take a long vacation!" George took Duke by the arm and headed to the trailer office. Duke was shaking his head in wonderment.

George parked the new Lincoln in the driveway, walked

to the front door, and called Nellie. She moved slowly, reluctantly. Outside in the driveway she walked around the car, giving each tire a sniff and wondering what it was all about.

George opened the passenger door and said: "Get in, Nellie. We are going for a ride!" She didn't need a second invitation and jumped up on the new leather seats with tail wagging wildly. George backed out of the driveway and headed toward their special place at the creek on the outskirts of town. He lowered the window; Nellie put her head into the wind. George looked at her and softly said, "This has to be a dog's prayer answered."

The Train Engineer

The train was moving fast and swayed to the left as it turned the bend and then slowed on the slight incline before entering the tunnel. Tom pushed the whistle button repeatedly as a warning signal that the train was approaching. The train shot out the far end of the tunnel and sped down the gradient again with the "toot, toot" sounding loudly.

Tom had his striped Santa Fe Railroad engineer's cap sitting a bit on the side of his head. He had trouble keeping it on straight and often wished he had been given a smaller size.

He slowed the train as it approached Farmerville Station and then brought it to a full stop at the station platform. The crossing gate was down, and the "ding, ding, ding" of the warning bell added to the excitement of running the train.

He pushed the whistle button three times and shouted loudly, "All aboard, all aboard; the train is leaving the station!"

The steam engine was red and silver with a black smoke funnel. "Jupiter" was printed in gold on the side of the coal tender. There were two passenger cars behind the engine--one yellow, the other dark red. The rest of the train consisted of a green freight car, a filled coal car, and a red caboose with a cupola on top.

"All aboard!" Tom shouted as the train pulled slowly away from the station platform. Down the track it sped past a farmhouse and a barn. Cows and horses were close to the track. Again, Tom hit the whistle button, "toot, toot, toot." As the train approached the tunnel grade, Tom's concentration was suddenly broken. Above the clickety clack of the engine wheels, he heard, "Tommy, it's time to turn off the train and come to lunch."

And They Say We Don't Know How to Cry

I could see him move along the tall weeds, at least I thought it was a "him." I didn't make a sound, but just kept my eyes on his movements. He obviously didn't see me as I was partially hidden by a tree trunk. He moved with caution and very slowly; he was stalking something. After a few minutes he came very close to where I was standing. I moved into the open, and was prepared for a confrontation if it came to that. He stopped abruptly and stared straight into my eyes. We were less than ten feet apart. Neither of us made a sound. Finally, I spoke with as much boldness as I could muster. "Who are you? What are you doing here? What do you want?"

"Take it easy, little lady, I won't bite. Which question do you want me to answer first?" He spoke with a strange softness. I became less concerned about what danger he posed.

"How about answering who you are?" He took a couple of steps toward me, but I held my ground. "People call me K.K. What's your name?" He took another step toward me, looking me straight in the eye.

"Never mind who I am. What are you doing here, and what do you want?"

He looked across the meadow toward the forest. "Lady, you wouldn't believe what I've been through."

I looked carefully at him, he seemed less intimidating, but he did look a little ragged and very thin for a fellow his size.

I softened my voice and tried to say as gently as I could, "Go ahead, tell me your story."

He again looked straight into my eyes, without a blink, and said, "You'd better sit down and get comfortable, because it'll take me some time to tell the whole story. By the way, who am I talking to?"

I hesitated a moment and then said, "My name is Piggy. Miss Piggy to you." I could see his look of disbelief.

"How in the world did you ever come by a name like that?"

I looked at him as menacingly as I could. "That's my name. I'm not asking for your approval. But if you must know, it was given to me by the kids I grew up with, and it stuck."

He took a couple more steps toward me and sat down on the ground. "I didn't mean any offense. Miss Piggy is a nice name. Do you mind if I just call you Piggy?"

"No, I don't mind. Now get on with your story."

"Well, to begin with, I live, or at least lived, in a room at a feed store in a little town that must be far from here. I am not even sure what direction it is, but it must be somewhere that way." He nodded west toward a low mountain range. "I had a really good place to live--good food, a good place to sleep, and not much to do all day. I only had to guard the place at night mostly to make sure that varmints didn't get into the feed store. I did a pretty good job; at least I was always getting compliments from the owner, Cindy. She really took good care of me and I did appreciate her kindness."

I got up, stretched, and settled down in a comfortable spot. This was obviously going to be a long story.

"Do you think I could have a drink of water and something to eat?" he asked, looking toward the deck at the back of the house.

I said, "Get on with your story first. I want to know what you are all about before I do any favors for you."

"O.K., I'll make it as short as I can. It won't be easy though. Well, since I was up most nights at Cindy's, I tended to sleep a lot during the day. Usually, when I fell asleep, nothing could wake me. About two months ago, near as I can tell, I was in the parking lot at the feed store. There was a pickup truck with a partly enclosed trailer parked in the lot. I guess a customer was inside buying something from Cindy. I looked in the trailer; there was a nice pile of clean straw on the floor. It was beginning to sprinkle a bit, so I crawled inside. With raindrops playing a lullaby on the roof, bam, I fell asleep in a split second. It was a dumb thing to do. I had a perfectly good bed inside the store, but I always liked being outside whenever I could, and that pile of straw looked real inviting." He stretched his back and looked directly at me. "Do you follow me so far?"

I said, "Yes, get on with it. I'll be called for dinner before long, and if you expect to get anything, you'd better tell me why you're here."

"Sorry, but I've had a terrible time over the past two months or so, and you're really the first person I've met who has shown any interest in me.

"To continue, I really fell into a deep sleep. The next thing I remember I was bumping along on a gravel road. The pickup and trailer had pulled out from the parking lot while I was asleep. I had no idea how long it'd been traveling. I looked out the rear of the trailer and didn't recognize a thing. I thought of jumping out, but it was moving too fast. I would've been killed for sure. I settled down. We drove on for a long time. We were really in the country. In a forest. The pickup slowed down, probably to avoid some pot holes, and I didn't hesitate. I jumped!"

He stood up for a moment then sat back down in the same spot. "I'd no idea what to do next. The pickup and trailer sped off in a cloud of dust. The driver obviously didn't know I had been back there, and he hadn't seen me when I jumped. Now, I wish he had. Maybe he would've taken me back to the feed store. But it was too late to think about that. I was going to have to figure out where I was and get back home on my own.

"Well, Piggy, I had a long time to regret my foolishness. I ended up sleeping the first night in a clearing in the forest. It was probably two or three miles from the spot where I jumped out of the trailer. It was cold, I was hungry, and to tell the truth, a little scared. Who could tell what wild animals were around. I couldn't be sure what to expect out in the middle of nowhere. Maybe the most frightening thing was I didn't know where I was, and wasn't at all sure what direction I should go. I'll tell you, I didn't sleep much that night. When the sun came up, I started walking. I spent most of the next day walking west. I figured that had to be the direction to go. By mid afternoon, I came upon a camper's tent. I was very hungry and sure I could smell food. I peeked in through the tent flap, but couldn't see anything that resembled something to eat. Just then I heard footsteps coming toward the tent out of the thick forest. I took off, but the guy with the footsteps saw me before I got very far and shouted for me not to run off. His voice seemed friendly enough. So I stopped and looked him over. He didn't appear to be angry at me for peering into the tent. Some people would really be upset and want to take you to task for lurking around regardless of your circumstances."

He again looked toward the deck of the house, stood up and stretched, sat down again, and continued. "Anyway, we made friends. He gave me one delicious meal. It turned out he was a fisherman and planned to camp in that spot for the next few weeks. He invited me to stay with him, if I wanted to. He sure liked to talk. He told me his life story--every day. He was some kind of big-time executive who came to the mountains to forget his miserable routine and all the pressures of his job. One good thing was, he seemed to have no interest in knowing where I came from or what I was doing there. So at least I wasn't answering questions. I didn't mind, as long as the food held out. When he went off to fish the river, I would tag along. I quite enjoyed it, actually. I'd find a flat rock to stretch out on in the sun and wait for lunch. He always brought enough for both of us.

"I stayed with him until he told me he was going to have to return to work. Obviously, he was doing so with regret. Although, he offered to take me to the city with him, I sure didn't plan on complicating my problems with that option. Every night he built a campfire, which I enjoyed. On the last night, before the fire died down, I took off. I didn't want to risk a long good-bye and take a chance of changing my mind and going off with him. My only interest was to get back to Cindy and my place in the feed store. So there I was. Lost, hungry, and feeling very sorry for myself, but sure I'd made the right decision."

He again stood and stretched. "Piggy, I'm cutting this story short, because right now I am very thirsty and starving. I hope you're satisfied enough with what I've told you to get me some water and something to eat."

"Yes," I said, "We'll give you food, but where have you been since leaving the fisherman?"

He gave a slight shrug and said, "For several weeks I was on a ranch, someplace back there." He pointed in the direction of the forest beyond the meadow. "I don't want to talk about it. I wasn't treated very well, although they did give me food and a place to sleep, even though it was in a barn and with a bunch of common farm cats. They kept me awake all night chasing mice around the barn. Then I spent some time at a house. People were seldom there and usually only at night. I felt like a scavenger. They did give me something to eat occasionally. One day they didn't return. I never saw them again. They really didn't have an interest in helping me. I don't think they wanted me around. I had several instances of that sort. And, here I am. You're really the first soul I've met to whom I could tell my story. Now can I have a drink of water and something to eat?"

I said, "Well, O.K. Let me go first and talk to Margaret. I think she'll give you something. Don't count on her allowing you to stay here, but she might do something to help you get home again."

I walked up the steps to the deck. Margaret was looking out the screen door. "Piggy, who's that you've been talking to?"

By that time, K.K. was already up the stairs and on the deck. He obviously looked hungry, as well as shabby, to Margaret. "Here, have some of this." She put a plate of food down in front of K.K. He didn't need an invitation. He dug in as though he hadn't eaten in a week. Maybe he hadn't. He turned to me and said, "This is the first time in a very long time I've been able to eat out of a proper dish and not some sort of paper plate, or worse. I really appreciate meeting up with you,

Miss Piggy. I will never forget you."

While K.K. was making short work of the dish of food, I could hear Margaret on the phone. She was talking to Cindy at the feed store. "Regarding your notice in the paper sometime ago...yes," she said. "He fits the description. We will be waiting for you." She described how to get to our place; and to the side, I heard her say, "Cindy is coming for him."

K.K. was unaware. About thirty minutes later, there was a knock at the front door. Margaret opened the door, and in walked Cindy. K.K. stood in silence; frozen in awe. In a flash he was in Cindy's arms. First Cindy closed her eyes as a few tears appeared, and then I noticed a tear dropped from K.K.'s eye. And they say we cats don't know how to cry!

Footnote:

Miss Piggy was a manx cat. She met K.K., but their meeting has been portrayed in a somewhat more friendly manner than was actually the case. Miss Piggy died at the ripe old age of 17.

She is buried with some of her favorite toys near our home in the woods. Her grave marker has an inscription: "Miss Piggy, 1980 - 1996, always our little friend."

K.K., also known as Kitty Kat, is happily doing his job keeping varmints out of Cindy's Feed Store in Granby, Colorado, often getting an affectionate pet from Cindy's customers. Although, K.K. still ventures outside when he pleases. He's now more cautious about where he chooses to sleep and into whose pickup or trailer he chooses to jump.

Eddie's Treasure

The early days of summer are always the best. School is out. Doing homework and being attentive, or at least pretending to be attentive, are forgotten. The joy of being free to walk along a creek and just to run to nowhere in particular push all thoughts of the school year into oblivion for 12-year-old Eddie Thorton. With Jam, his faithful beagle mixture, he would spend the early days of summer in the peaceful shade of oak trees along the little-used trail at Catfish Creek. While it was referred to as a, creek, in several places along its path, the thin stream of slowly moving water simply disappeared to be seen again a distance downstream.

Today was the third day of summer vacation, and the feeling of newly found freedom was still glowing in Eddie. With Jam at his side, they ran together, then slowed to a walk along the trail. Jam would cover twice the distance of Eddie, running around trees and through the thin creek stream lapping up water in big gulps.

Jam was named by Eddie's father when they picked him out of a line-up at the city pound three years before. His father said the little mongrel was "Just A Mutt," and the initials stuck. Jam was totally faithful to Eddie and suffered greatly when Eddie was gone all day long every week of the school year.

Today, on the third day of vacation, a short distance down the path along Catfish Creek, Jam stopped to sniff an object sticking out of a tangle of dead twigs. Eddie bent over to get a closer look at whatever it was that caught Jam's attention. At first glance, Eddie thought it was a piece of foil or a wadded-up gum wrapper. No, it was much more than that! He picked up a metal disk and rubbed it clean of dirt and dust. It was about two inches in diameter and had ornate embossing on both sides. He unsnapped a catch, and the inside was clean and very shiny but empty. He knew it was a locket. His mother had one that was similar in size but clearly not as ornate. This *was* a treasure!

His outing with Jam was cut short. They headed directly home, the treasure held tightly in Eddie's closed fist. He took a Diamond Brand match stick box from his dresser drawer, removed three rubber bands that kept it closed to possible intruders, dumped out the once-precious collection of three coins, four pebbles, and two feathers. He blew dust from inside the box and carefully placed his new treasure in a wad of cotton and back in the box, again securing it with three rubber bands.

The rest of the day, Eddie opened and reopened the match box to stare at his treasure. He thought to himself, "This is the best thing I have ever found in my entire life. I'm going to keep it forever." He put the box in several different hiding places, always afraid it would be discovered.

That evening, Eddie could no longer contain his secret. He took the box to his mother and carefully undid the rubber bands. "Look, Mom; Jam and I found this on the creek path this morning. I think it must be very valuable. It is, isn't it?"

"Oh! It's a silver locket." His mother put on her glasses

and took the locket from Eddie. Turning it over, she spotted small engraved symbols. "There are hallmarks. It is silver. Yes, Eddie, I think it may well be valuable."

Eddie was filled with excited pleasure. "What's a hallmark?" he asked.

"Look here," Eddie's mother pointed to the small, etched marks on the back of the locket. "These indicate if it is silver and where and when it was made. Maybe you should take it down to Edith Johnson and ask her about it. She works at the City Museum and might be able to tell its worth. I must say, it does look old." His mother handed the locket back to Eddie.

Eddie's heart was pounding. His precious find *was* a valuable treasure! "O.K., we'll go ask her. Come on, Jam." The two of them half ran to the front door and down the street to the Johnson's house a half block away.

Eddie rang the doorbell. Mrs. Johnson appeared at the door on the third hurried ring. "Yes, Eddie, what can I do for you?"

He quickly undid the rubber bands, held the locket up, and said: "Look, Mrs. Johnson! Jam and I found this on the creek path this morning...."

Before he could continue, Mrs. Johnson took the locket from Eddie's hand, held it to her breast. "Oh, how wonderful! You found it! I've looked for this for ages. I didn't know where I lost it. Thank you ever so much, Eddie." She bent down, gave a bewildered and disappointed Eddie a tight hug, and patted Jam on the head.

The Sixth
Letter Home

Letter No. 1
Le Havre, France
1 January 1945

Dear Mom and Dad,

We arrived early this morning at the Port of Le Havre, France. It took a long time to get us all off the ship, but everyone is off now and ready to go. I will number my letters from now on, at least while I am over here. That will make sure you can figure out the sequence. Also, I'm not sure I will always be able to tell what the date is. I lost track of the days and dates coming over here. This morning I mailed all the letters I wrote you on board the troopship. I wrote every day. There really wasn't much else to do. Most of the boys played cards or read books or comics.

Landing in France is a disappointment for most of us. We were told we would disembark in England for more training, but someplace along the way the brass decided to send us directly to a "repple depot" here in France. They call the replacement camps, "repple depots." I was hoping to be able to sightsee around England before we got into action, but I guess that isn't going to happen.

After we disembarked about 07:00, we boarded
trucks but only went about three miles to an open field with
tents and stacks upon stacks of equipment, artillery pieces,
trucks, and tanks and stacks of oil drums all lined up as far
as we could see. Now we are sitting around on our duffel
bags waiting for somebody to do something.

Even though it is boring to be just sitting around, I
am very happy to be off that troopship. I won't write the
name of the ship, because I'm sure the censors will cut it
out. (We have been told not to write place names or
locations where we are. They will probably cut out the
name "Le Havre.") Anyway, that ship really stunk. I spent
as much time as I could on deck in the fresh sea air. The
quarters really smelled. For a farm boy from Iowa, you
would think I could put up with the odor, but I can tell you
there isn't anything on our farm that would even come
close.

New Year's Eve was pretty uneventful. A chaplain
said mass at midnight, the same as Christmas Eve. There
wasn't much celebrating. We had to maintain blackout
conditions, and I think everyone was worried that there
might be Nazi subs or mines floating around as we got
closer to land. I know I was.

It looks like we will be spending the night here. At
least there are tents, cots, a field mess, and especially
decent latrines. It is pretty cold, so it is good to see some
barracks tents. It is really overcast. I guess that is a good
thing, because every now and then we can hear airplanes
over our heads and can't be sure if they are ours or the
Germans. We can hear explosions once in awhile. They
are probably bombs dropping somewhere along the coast.
There was a lot of antiaircraft fire too. It's surprising to
hear the noise coming from a spot close by us, but we can

hardly see where they are because they are so well camouflaged. I'm not sure they know what they are firing at. It is impossible to see anything through the overcast. They might even be firing at our own planes! There are plenty of barrage balloons in the sky. I don't think the German planes would attempt to get below the clouds. If they do, they will run into ropes or wires hanging from the barrage balloons which are all along the coast.

I think everyone is a little scared. No one knows what is coming next. People talk a lot to one another, probably out of nervousness. We are all in the same boat. I haven't met anyone who has been through this before.

I have to tell you that some guys aboard ship made fun of me because my military serial number has an "RA" in front, meaning regular army and meaning that I enlisted. The draftees poke fun, saying I found a home in the army and would re-up or re-enlist when my enlistment was up. I don't care; I'm proud to be in uniform and know that I'm doing my part to defeat the Nazis. Most of the boys I was with in basic training were enlistees, but I didn't see very many on board. They must have been assigned to other ships. There were plenty of troopships around leaving about the same time as ours.

I will close for now. It looks like they are calling a formation. Give old Polly a pet for me. I miss my dog.

Love, Billy

+—+ ≡◆≡ —+

Letter No. 2
Somewhere in Belgium
2 January 1945

Dear Mom and Dad,

This is going to be a short letter. I'm writing while we are making a rest stop. We stayed in the repple depot over night. Had a good hot breakfast this morning at 04:00, loaded on troop transport trucks, and have been traveling ever since. Unfortunately, I was assigned to a truck without a canopy, and it has been very cold. But the good thing is, I can see the countryside.

We have gone through some villages that have been leveled by bombs and artillery shells, but we have also passed through towns that haven't been touched. They look very old and very picturesque. After the war I'd like to come back here for a visit. Every village, no matter how small, has a church, but most of the steeples are gone. One of the guys sitting next to me said that our tanks and artillery shoot at them because it's where the German snipers and artillery observers usually hang out.

Most of the towns we have gone through are smaller than Dyersville, about the size of Centerville. There is plenty of wrecked equipment along the road--American, British, and German. In places it looks like a long junkyard. But the saddest thing to see is the number of dead animals, mostly cows and horses. They are everywhere, and the smell is pretty bad. I suppose many were killed by concussion from bombs and shells. Maybe the Germans killed some to lessen the food supply they left behind. I imagine there were also bodies of people, but they would have been taken away and buried by now.

The convoy stopped twice. We had to jump out of

the trucks and run to road-side ditches because of low-flying aircraft. I think they were ours both times, but couldn't really tell. They went by very fast, and we were told to keep our heads down. Anyway, there were no bombs or machine-gun fire. They were either ours or Germans who had run out of ammunition.

We are being ordered to load up and move out. I will write tomorrow when we get to wherever we are going. Give Polly a pet for me.

Love, Billy

<hr>

Letter No. 3
Somewhere in Belgium
3 January 1945

Dear Mom and Dad,

We finally got to a stopping point. Out of the 30 or 40 trucks in the convoy that started with us, there are only four left. The others have turned off in different directions along the way. I've seen several town names, but I won't write them down because I know the censors will cut them out anyway. It seems like we have been traveling forever. Every bone in my body aches. It has been a rough ride hitting potholes and bomb debris. We have been ordered to disembark and leave all our personal gear in the equipment trailers we have been towing. That means our duffel bags, bedrolls, and everything else. We can take only our rifle, water canteen, gas mask, and the rations they gave us in the repple depot.

There is some sergeant who gave us a lecture on

what we can expect over the next few days. He had a really scarred face and looked very tough. I don't believe half the stuff he said. I think they only want to scare us so we keep on our toes and obey orders. He said, "Welcome to the Battle of the Bulge," whatever that is.

We have been told we will march about five miles to a defensive post. We are replacements. I have been assigned to a rifle squad. One of the NCOs, who was waiting for us, is in charge of our squad. His name is Corporal Pappas. He is from Pennsylvania and is really old, maybe even as old as you, Dad. Somebody said he heard that Corporal Pappas was in the first World War and held a high rank--maybe even an officer. He stayed in the army after the war and apparently got into trouble and was demoted to corporal. He seems like the sort of guy who would tell a superior officer to go jump in the lake if he didn't agree with him. Anyway, they call him Pappy. I think he is even older than you, Dad.

Pappy said we have to march to his defensive line because the troop carriers would draw German artillery fire if they saw them moving down the road. The trucks are supposed to bring our duffel bags and bedrolls to our position after dark.

We have been marching for over an hour. I'm writing this during a break. We passed five German tanks just parked along the road. They weren't damaged. Pappy said they probably ran out of gas, and the crews just abandoned them and then hiked back to Germany. We were told not to go into them as they could be booby-trapped. We were also told to stay alert in case the crews didn't hike back to Germany and were hiding in the woods along the road. By this time, I am glad they didn't allow us to bring our personal gear. I am tired just carrying my rifle, gas mask, and rations. I hated to leave Uncle Ed's camera in my duffel bag, but I'm sure it will be O.K.

We have had to take cover three times because of planes flying over. There were no bombs and no shooting, but we had to get off the road just in case. I am wet and muddy. The last time we had to take cover, I fell into a ditch with a coat of ice, but the ice broke when I landed on it. Now I am really cold.

I saw one of the planes, but couldn't tell if it was ours or theirs. We had some plane identification classes in basic, but looking at pictures is a lot different than looking at the real thing. I am not alone. Some guys said they were German Messerschmitts, and some said they were our fighters. We are getting ready to move out again, so I will close. Give Polly a pet.

Love, Billy

━━◆━━

Letter No. 4
Somewhere in Belgium
4 January 1945

Dear Mom and Dad,

We got to the defensive line yesterday afternoon. I was assigned to a foxhole along the road. There are dozens of foxholes all about the same distance apart--about as far as it is from our back door to the chicken coup.

The foxhole I was assigned was occupied by Pfc. Mike McMahon. He said I owe him because he had to dig the foxhole by himself. I told him I could make it bigger, but he said the smaller the better in case there is a German 88 artillery barrage. Mike is a nice guy. He comes from a town in the Colorado Rocky Mountains. It sounds like a very pretty place. He was also sent here as a replacement. We talk a lot.

It is boring and very cold sitting in this foxhole. Earlier today, a few of us left our foxholes and got into a barn about 30 yards away, just to try and warm up. The platoon sergeant found us there and really chewed us out. He told us to get back to our foxholes and stay there. He told me to keep my helmet on because my red hair would make a perfect target for a German sniper. Mike said that Sergeant Williams was in the second landing wave at someplace in France called Omaha Beach on "D" Day in early June. He landed as a private, but all the NCOs in his battalion were casualties along the way getting to here. Williams was promoted to staff sergeant. They call him the "old man," but he is only 21 years old.

A little while ago, I saw three German soldiers being escorted to a prisoner compound by a GI. They walked along the road right in front of me. I got a good look at them. I told Mike that they didn't look old enough to shave. He said to me: "Look who's talking. Red, you don't look old enough to be in the Boy Scouts." I told him: "Number one, I am going to be 19 on the 7th of January; and two, I don't like to be called 'Red.'" He was only kidding around, and we have talked so much about ourselves I feel I have known him for a long time.

There really is nothing to do except to try and keep warm and look across a field toward a treeline which is about as far away as the back fence on the south forty--maybe even a mile. It is hard to guess because it is so foggy and overcast.

I hope our duffel bags and bedrolls show up soon. I nearly froze to death last night. I also hope they bring up the field kitchens. C-rations are terrible. You have to be very hungry to eat them.

This is turning out to be a long letter. I don't have anything else to do. We watch for any movement across the way in the woods but haven't seen a thing. We can hear a constant hum of bombers flying overhead but can't see them with all the fog and cloud cover. Every time someone gets out of their foxhole, Sergeant Williams shouts for them to get down and then he shouts a lot of cuss words, letting everyone know that stupid stunts like that will draw an 88-artillery barrage and get us all killed.

A little while ago, a jeep pulled up near us. There was a full-bird colonel, a driver, a sergeant, and a dog that looked a lot like Polly. That's the first colonel I've seen close up since I've been in the army. They parked the jeep right near us. What a target for the Germans, but Sergeant Williams didn't say a word. They unrolled a map on the hood of the jeep. The dog just sat by the colonel's feet and looked like he was just as important as the rest of them. After a few minutes, the sergeant started walking down the road. He must be a forward artillery spotter. The jeep turned around and headed back the direction it came from.

You know, Dad, after seeing all the dead animals, I think I will become a veterinarian when I get out of the army. Corporal Pappas said we can get college paid for through the GI bill. I hope so. I really would like to become a vet instead of a farmer.

It seems like I've been writing this bit by bit all

afternoon. It is something to keep occupied. I'm still very cold. My feet feel like pieces of ice. Some boys have been sent back to an evacuation hospital with severe frostbite or trench foot. Still no duffel bags or bedrolls or hot meals. Right now, I would settle for a blanket. I'm not sure about this army stuff. As I sit here, I wonder why I am here.

    It's dead quiet. Once in awhile, we can hear artillery from far away. Last night we saw flares to the south, but don't know whose they were or why. I haven't yet seen a German except the prisoners walking by. I haven't fired my rifle once. There is ice on it. I hope I can fire it if I have to. A few days ago, you could see yourself in it, I had polished it so much. Now it doesn't look so good.

    My birthday is in a couple of days, and I don't want a cake with candles. I just want a hot bath, some clean clothes, and a hot meal; but I don't suppose I will get any of them.

    We haven't had a mail call since landing. Maybe I'll get your letters tomorrow. It is getting hard to see, so I will close for now. Give Polly a pet for me.

        Love, Billy

P.S.: We have just heard from Pappy that the colonel's jeep hit a land mine and killed the colonel, driver, and the dog. I sure hope it wasn't one of our mines.

—•—▨◆▨—•—

Letter No. 5
Somewhere in Belgium
5 January 1945

Dear Mom and Dad,

Please don't worry about me. I have to dictate this letter for my friend Mike to write. We are in a field hospital. I have some shrapnel in me and can't sit up. Give Polly a pet for me.

Love, Billy

Dear Mr. and Mrs. Brady,

I am taking the liberty of finishing Billy's letter to let you know that during the night we were hit by an 88-artillery barrage. One shell hit a barn near our foxhole and started a big fire. A little later another hit close to us and knocked both of us out. Billy caught a lot of fragments, and I got some in the leg. He does not seem to be in pain; he has been heavily sedated and is sleeping now. I will help him write you again tomorrow. I am supposed to go into surgery early in the morning.

Yours truly,
Michael T. McMahon, Pfc

P.S.: Billy doesn't know that Corporal Pappas was killed during the barrage. I know he thought a lot of Pappy.

＊＋ ☰＋☰ ＋＊

Letter No. 6
Somewhere in Belgium
6 January 1945
Dear Mr. and Mrs. Brady,

I'm sure you will have heard from the War Department before receiving this letter that Billy died of his wounds. The chaplain came by to see how I was doing, and I told him I would be writing to you. He asked that I tell you that he is Father Kelly and that he said Mass this morning in the ward close to Billy's bed. After Mass, he gave Billy the Last Rites, and Billy died with a slight smile on his face. I'm sure he was thinking of you two and his dog, Polly. I hope I can stop by to visit with you on my way back to Colorado. I would really like to meet you, and I would like to give Polly a pet for Billy. I am looking forward to meeting you.

Sincerely yours,
mike

Footnote:
On January 7, a crippled American B-17 bomber attempting a forced landing, struck the field hospital killing most doctors, nurses, Chaplain Kelly, most patients, and Pfc. Michael T. McMahon.

Road Hands

After World War II, during the 1950s, a considerable amount of state and Federal funding was provided for road building: paving, realignment of old roads, and construction of new roads and new bridges. Although it was a nationwide effort, road construction in New Mexico was a major undertaking statewide.

The state was poor and sparsely populated. During the 1930s and 1940s very little money was spent on road improvements. Most of the roads throughout the state were gravel, at best. Although national highways 85 and 66 were paved, both were just two lanes. For several years following the war, road construction accounted for much of New Mexico's employment base, which really didn't say much for the level of employment in the rest of the businesses or industries in the state.

Construction workers were generally qualified. Most had been in WW II and were well trained by the Navy as Seabees (a phonetic acronym for "Construction Battalion") or by the Army Engineers. These were rough and tough individuals, who were independent; many hadn't lost the hard lessons learned from their farm or ranch upbringing. As a group, they were "diamonds in the rough."

Following are stories of some of the more memorable incidents from that time.

B. M. Petersen and Sonny Kean

Bernard M. Petersen was a tough foreman for Moran & Floyd Construction Company. He was in charge of a new road project a few miles east of Reserve, New Mexico. New hires were told to call him "B. M." and never Bernard. Petersen had been in the Navy Seabees for three or four years. Before he enlisted in the Navy, he was a drifting New Mexico cowboy. Although he could often be heard saying, "The only thing the Navy taught me was not to pee into the wind," he did, however, learn a management style while in the Navy; and it was not particularly appreciated by other "road hands." "Road hand" was a term commonly applied to anyone who worked in road construction: laborers, cat skinners, motor grader operators, scraper operators, and powder monkeys. Many of the construction workers still held resentment for the frequently occurring orders they received from authoritative, noncommissioned officers, regardless of the branch of service. To them, B. M. was a noncom. They would follow his orders but still didn't like it.

Sonny Kean held a particularly deep resentment for authority. It dated back six or seven years to when he was a Seabee constructing airfields on Pacific islands, sometimes while under sniper fire. Japanese soldiers seldom retreated nor surrendered and often hid in nearby jungles taking pot shots at GIs building bases and airfields. Sonny could not hold on to a promotion. He had been promoted to petty officer on three occasions and also demoted on three occasions; he was demoted for fighting with fellow Seabees. All his fights occurred during nights of heavy drinking. He was a better-than-average scraper operator and couldn't be spared from building urgently needed airfields, so he never spent time in the brig. He was essential to the effort. After his discharge from the Navy, Sonny wasn't essential to anything and, after heavy drinking and fighting, had spent a few nights in various jails around New Mexico.

B. M. Petersen was a particular irritant for Sonny. He recognized in B. M. every noncom he hated in the Navy. Sonny constantly argued with B. M. over any instruction, suggestion, or order concerning the way he operated the scraper. On payday, always on Friday, Sonny looked at his pocketwatch. At exactly five o'clock, quitting time, Sonny drove his scraper at top speed to the timekeeper's shack. He would race anyone foolish enough to challenge him, whether they were in another scraper, a truck, or a pickup.

After a hard day of dust, sun, and wind, Sonny watched as B. M. passed the scraper, leaving him to cough in a cloud of dust. B. M. had recently taken delivery of a new Dodge pickup. The dust, the sight of the new pickup, and overall resentment of B. M., mixed with a two-day hangover, caused rage in Sonny. As he approached the construction yard, he saw Petersen's pickup truck parked at the shack door. Sonny just couldn't contain himself. He drove the heavy scraper at full speed over the new Dodge pickup. The six-foot, earth-mover tire crushed the right side of Petersen's pickup. Sonny turned the engine off, jumped down from the operator's cab, and swaggered into the timekeepers office.

"Gimme my check; I quit." He looked at the shocked B. M. Petersen. "You know what B. M. stands for, don't you, Bernard? Well, you're the biggest B. M. I have ever known!"

Sonny wasn't seen again but probably went to another part of the state and hired on as a scraper operator for some unsuspecting construction company.

B. M. Petersen didn't report the incident. He knew the sheriff wouldn't do anything. The sheriff, police, and judge just endured the road hands in the area, waiting for them to finish construction and move on to some other hapless jurisdiction.

Curley Crammer

Curley was a tough cat skinner. The term "cat skinner" had origins dating back to the early 1900s or maybe even the 1800s during construction of embankments for railroads. The teamster would snap a whip above mules to keep them pulling earth scrapers or wagons loaded with earth and rock. They were called "mule skinners." As mules were replaced by diesel-powered, crawler tractors made by the Caterpillar Tractor Company, the term applied to the drivers was "cat skinner."

The Green Brothers Construction Company was low bidder on a road construction project south of Alamagordo, New Mexico. Curley was hired to run one of the Green Brothers Caterpillar bulldozers. To most people, Curley appeared not to have a fear in the world. Secretly, he had a terrifying fear of snakes.

Winters in southern New Mexico can't be compared to winters in the north, but nights can reach freezing temperatures. At dawn on a clear December morning, Curley cranked up the starting engine to warm up the bulldozer engine. It took several minutes to get it started. The night before had been cold and close to freezing. Curley climbed up on the crawler tracks and jumped into the operator's seat, unaware of the Red Racer snake tightly coiled on the transmission cover between Curley's feet. In all likelihood, the snake was attracted by the residual warmth in the transmission from the previous day's operation. The Red Racer uncoiled and shot to Curley's right boot, went straight up his leg, under his belt, under his shirt, and curled around his neck.

Curley let out a scream and jumped from the bulldozer seat to the ground, yelling, "Snake! Snake! Get if off me!"

He didn't need help. By the time Curley hit the ground, running in a circle, he had managed to pull the snake off his neck and slung it away in a high arc. It landed in the weeds.

Curley stood shaking and cursing. He was so excited, he couldn't stop jabbering. "It was a snake! Did you see that? It was a snake! It was strangling me around the neck!"

In the weeds, the Red Racer regained composure and raced back to Curley's right boot, went straight up his leg, under his belt, under his shirt, and curled around his neck. Curley screamed, "It's back! Help! Get if off me! Help!"

He didn't need help. In a split second, the Red Racer was flying through the air back to the weeds; and Curley was running for his pickup. His workday was over.

Curley was not influenced as the foreman explained the Red Racer was just looking for a nice warm place and was harmless in any case. No matter what the foreman said, Curley's workday was over. He spent the rest of the day and much of the night in Jack's Bar in Alamogordo.

Terry Cord

Winter was a difficult time for road hands in New Mexico. Road construction projects in the state were often delayed by sudden snowstorms; and when a road hand wasn't working, he didn't get paid. Worse, on idle days, they would often squander their time in one bar or another spending the last weeks' wages. Snow days were equally hard on the wives of road hands. They would see the rent money squandered on beer, tavern shuffleboard games, music juke boxes, or lost in poker games. They would also lay awake in bed until one or two o'clock in the morning waiting for their booze-happy husbands to come home.

Terry Cord looked forward to snowy days when the state highway engineer would tell the contractor to shut the project down because of snow. It never took him long to park his front end loader and head for Crazy Mary's Bar and Restaurant in Tucumcari.

On one such snowy March day, he burst through the barroom door shouting, "Hey, Crazy Mary, give me a Four Roses bourbon and Seven-up! Drinks for everybody on me!" It was ten-thirty in the morning.

By eleven o'clock that night, Terry felt no pain and would have had one more drink for the road; but he had spent every cent he had. Crazy Mary didn't believe in credit, especially not for road hands.

She tried to talk Terry into getting a motel room and staying the night in Tucumcari, telling him he was in no shape to drive the 30 miles to his trailer park. He wouldn't hear of it.

Weaving back and forth, he slurred the words, "Margo is waiting for me. I'll bet she's keeping supper warm. I've got to get home."

The snow was letting up, but the wind was building drifts across the highway. Terry had trouble keeping his eyes open. Alcohol and the blur of drifting snow lulled him to sleep. His pickup swerved to the right and hit a bridge abutment and was sent rolling down a steep embankment. The pickup overturned several times and ended up on its top in a snowdrift. Terry was thrown out the driver's side on the first rollover. He was free of the pickup but lifeless in two feet of snow.

The next morning, Margo was doing the week's laundry in the trailer park laundromat. Deputy Sheriff Jasper Slade walked into the laundry shed. "Hi, Jasper, what brings you out here? Terry isn't home. I suppose he stayed in town last night because of the snowstorm. You'd think the bum would at least have called the trailer park office to let me know. Maybe he did. Those people never deliver messages."

Jasper Slade had been friends of the Cords for many years. "Margo, it's about Terry." Slade spoke in a whisper. "I'm afraid I have very bad news. Terry ran off the road sometime last night halfway between here and town. He was found in the snow about eight this morning. There was nothing that could be done for him. I'm real sorry. They have him in the morgue at county hospital. We need you to identify his body."

Margo Cord rocked from side to side, holding her hand over her mouth, trying to grasp what Slade was telling her. "No, Jasper. No, it can't be! It can't be!" She broke into quick sobs. Slade put his arm around Margo to steady her.

"Come, Margo, I'll drive you to the hospital. I'm real sorry."

The county coroner was in the small basement room of the hospital which served as the county morgue. He was standing next to a gurney as Margo and Deputy Slade walked in. He lifted a white sheet covering Terry Cord's head. He looked at Margo and in a somber tone said, "Is this your husband, Mr. Terry Cord, Mrs. Cord?"

Margo gasped as she looked at Terry's head. It appeared that his scalp had come loose from his skull and was sitting at a slight angle on his head.

"Oh! Good Lord! Yes, it's Terry! Oh, how horrible!" She broke into tears as she looked down at the body.

In a shade of a moment, she exclaimed, "He's not dead. Look! There are tears running down his cheek!"

The coroner quickly bent over Terry, and said, "You're right; he is alive! Jasper, quick, help me get the gurney to the elevator. We don't have a second to lose!"

Terry Cord had spent nine hours in freezing temperatures, covered with snow. When he was thrown from the pickup, his head hit the open door, and his scalp was peeled away from his skull. The doctor later told Margo the combination of the cold and alcohol probably saved Terry's life.

Terry recovered with no lasting effects. He was a changed person. He never returned to Crazy Mary's Bar and never again went to a tavern without Margo. When he did, he usually ordered a glass of milk.

Jess Gonzales

Over the days, months, and years, road hands developed strong feelings for fellow workers. At times, it was nearly impossible for a stranger to be included in that fellowship. New employees on a road construction job would be ignored and seldom included in conversations, even during the noon lunch breaks.

Jess Gonzales was hired as a water-truck driver. His job was to keep the roadbed moist while the motor grader operator shifted the bed surface to conform to grade stakes. He had been hired by Coe and Son Contractors shortly after the company was awarded a street-building contract by the village of Grants, New

Mexico. Grants had Route 66 on the north side of town and the Santa Fe Railroad on the south side. There were only a few blocks between the two.

At lunch break, the grader operator, roller operator, three laborers, the foreman, and Jess Gonzales gathered under a cottonwood tree. Each had nearly identical black lunch pails and a Thermos bottle. A conversation developed, but it was apparent that Jess was not included. During a lull in the discussion, Jess spoke up. "Are any of you guys interested in buying a surplus Army Jeep?"

Albert, the foreman, was first to break the ensuing silence. "Wha'dya mean, Gonzales? What are you talking about--surplus Army Jeep?"

Jess was pleased that the foreman knew his name. He took on an air of seriousness, "I have an uncle who handles Army surplus from the Korean War. He said he is getting some surplus jeeps that are brand new, never used, still in cosmoline, and in the original crates. He asked if I wanted one. The government says he has to resell them at a set price."

"How much?" the roller operator asked.

"Yeah, how much?" one of the laborers joined in.

Jeff hesitated a moment and said, "He has to sell them for $200 apiece. He has no choice. He said I have to pay the railroad freight from Houston to get it here if I want one."

"Two hundred dollars! For a new Jeep! I'll take one," the motor-grader operator shouted.

The rest of the lunch group joined in, saying they also wanted one. Jess and his Jeeps was the only topic of conversation for the rest of the lunch hour. He turned down offers of money and down payments of $20 and $50. Albert even offered to give Jess $200 from his wallet on the spot.

Jess basked in his popularity. He explained he didn't want the money until he knew the Jeeps were on a freight car and headed to Grants. He said he would call his uncle that very evening and order a Jeep for each of his new-found friends.

As word of the two-hundred-dollar Jeeps spread among the road hands on the construction site, Jess became the most talked about, talked to, and respected employee of the Coe and Son Contracting Company. He had taken orders for 17 Army surplus Jeeps; and with each new order, he swore the buyer to secrecy.

"My uncle does not want this deal to be spread around. He might get into trouble with the surplus people, so keep it to yourself," he would tell each expectant buyer.

Jess would receive greetings from company workers no matter where he went--in bars, at church, even at the grocery store. He would often be introduced to his co-workers wives and children. Jess had never been so popular.

The second week after he had made the Jeep announcement, Albert, the foreman, flagged Jess down while he was slowly watering the road bed. "Jess, I want to give you my $200 now before the old lady spends it on new furniture. Here." He tried to hand Jess two one-hundred-dollar bills.

Jess responded, "I can't take your money yet, Albert." Of late, he and Albert were on first-name terms. "Don't worry; I will let you know the exact amount I have to pay my uncle as soon as he tells me they are on the way and what the freight charge is."

Albert put the bills back in his wallet. "Do you know when your uncle is going to ship them, Jess?"

"No, but I will call him this evening and find out what the story is." Jess started the water-truck engine and continued sprinkling water on the roadbed, singing slightly off key, "Oh, what a beautiful morning, oh what a beautiful day; I've got a beautiful feeling; everything's going my way."

Another week passed. After work, Albert sought out Jess as he parked the water truck in the construction compound. "Hey, Jess, the boys are getting anxious for their Jeeps. What have you heard from your uncle?"

"I talked to my uncle last night. He gave me the freight-car numbers. I think they should arrive here in a couple of weeks." Jess gave Albert a slap on the back. "You guys should be driving your Jeeps around here by the end of the month."

Albert suggested: "What do you say we go down to the freight depot and see if the agent can tell us anything? He should know how long it might take for them to get here. He might even be able to trace the boxcars."

"Ah, O.K., Albert. I'll have to go back to my room to get the freight-car numbers."

"I'll drive you there." Albert pointed to his pickup truck parked behind the construction company's office trailer.

The two of them drove to Jess's room at a highway motel. Jess was gone for several minutes; and when he came out of the motel room, he waved a piece of paper to Albert. "Here they are, Albert!"

They drove up to the freight office and showed the list of numbers to the agent. "I don't recognize any of these numbers. I think you'd better get a copy of the bill of lading. I'll need that before I can help you." The agent handed the list of car numbers back to Jess.

"I'll call my uncle again tonight," Jess said to Albert as they drove back to the construction yard for Jess to get his car. Albert let him out and said: "See you in the morning, Jess. Be sure to call your uncle and let me know what he says." As Albert drove off, Jess turned to go into the construction company's trailer office.

The next morning, Albert went to the office and spoke to the timekeeper. "Have you seen Jess this morning? He isn't on the job. His water truck is still parked."

The timekeeper replied, "Why, Albert, I thought you knew. Jess picked up his pay last night and quit. He's gone. He didn't mention where he was headed."

Albert pursed his lips and walked out the door. He couldn't hide his disappointment as he realized there weren't going to be any two-hundred dollar Army surplus Jeeps; he thought to himself, "That dog Jess probably doesn't even have an uncle in Houston."

Guy Swift

The Rock Island Railroad tracks and the Southern Pacific tracks meet at a point about one mile west of Santa Rosa, New Mexico. There is no marker, and the exact connecting point couldn't be identified without a right-of-way survey. However, it was generally assumed the connecting spot was at the bottom of the grade. It really didn't matter where it was except for the maintenance crews who were very careful not to do repairs to one another's tracks.

Guy Swift was timekeeper for the J. J. Beck Constructors, with head offices in Albuquerque. The company secured a contract to build a new railroad bridge over Route 66 on the west side of Santa Rosa. The project called for a two-mile-long shoofly, which is a railroad detour. In order to build the shoofly, it was necessary to have heavy, earthmoving machinery close to the tracks. The station master in the Santa Rosa depot warned the company that it was absolutely necessary that equipment be kept ten feet away from the tracks and moved at least fifteen minutes before a train would pass the construction site. He explained that trains going either east or west would be reaching top speed down the grade in order to gain momentum to go up the opposite grade. He also pointed out that, since the Rock Island Limited daily passenger train didn't stop in Santa Rosa, it would be going full speed, maybe even the fastest it traveled anywhere on the route.

It was up to the contracting company to know the train schedules and assure that no equipment was near the tracks when the trains were due. It was Swift's responsibility to get the daily schedules and advise the construction foreman. He always worried about getting correct information and making sure the foreman acted promptly in pulling the earth-moving machinery back from the tracks. He often visualized a major train disaster if procedures were not diligently followed.

Over the months of construction, he made sure there were no mistakes and no mishaps. He was happy to see the project completed without a problem as far as the railroad was concerned.

The next project the company was awarded was in Aztec, New Mexico. The job required earth fill which had to be moved by earthmovers across the Denver & Rio Grande Western railroad tracks at a crossing a mile or two north of Aztec.

On a quiet Monday morning, Swift was at his desk in the office trailer making out payroll records when the foreman opened the office door and shouted that one of the earthmovers had ripped up the DRGW tracks at the crossing.

Swift went into an uncontrolled panic as he shouted back, "When is the next train due?"

The foreman fired back, "How the hell should I know! Get down to the depot and tell them! There could be a train on the way right now. If there is, it will be one helluva wreck. The tracks look like spaghetti!"

Thoughts of the last project and the Rock Island Line went through Swift's head. He had to move fast. There could be a major disaster. He could visualize a wreck with railcars scattered about the crossing.

Guy Swift jumped into his pickup truck, spun the rear wheels, and drove at top speed toward the DRGW depot. As he arrived at the depot, he didn't bother to close the pickup truck door, left the engine running, and hurried into the depot office.

The agent looked up through a green eye shade. "What can I do for you, son?"

Swift shouted, "The track is out north of town! A scraper dropped its bucket at the crossing and ripped the tracks out. Quick, when's the next train due? Hurry! You have to warn them!"

The agent calmly looked at Swift, "Take it easy. Let's see, that schedule is on my desk somewhere. Ah, here it is." He casually fingered the pages and said, "Let's see, today is Monday and . . . "

Swift couldn't contain himself. His fears were at the edge of his mind. "For God's sake, man! Would you hurry! There is a disaster in the making! If you can't read that damn thing, give it to me!"

The agent turned pages in the schedule and said, "Take it easy, sonny. So, today is Monday. Hmmm, it looks like the next train is due through here...maybe a week from Friday. Now, does that satisfy you? I'll advise maintenance, and they'll have it fixed in no time at all. By the way, thanks for letting me know."

Swift sat down on a lobby chair, put his head in his hands, and sobbed. He was sure that the episode had taken years off his life. It seemed that the DRGW only ran one or two trains a month to Aztec, very slowly at that.

Swede Johnson and a "Sinking Feeling"

During the mid-1950s, Americans were experiencing a time of comfort and prosperity. After years of depression misery, World War II, and the Korean War, the peacefulness of the 1950s was much appreciated. Families were able to afford first cars and even new cars and were quick to use them to travel throughout the country, especially to the West.

This brings me to my story about Swede and a sinking feeling. At the time, I was in the road and street-contracting business in New Mexico. Our company would bid with very aggressive prices on nearly any state highway project that was advertised, and we thought we hit real pay dirt when we were the low bidder and awarded a project on Route 66 entering the town of Santa Rosa, New Mexico.

Route 66 was well known. It was so well known, it became the subject of a popular television series at the time called "Route 66." It was an adventure story about two fellows who toured the route from coast to coast in a sleek Chevy Corvette. Route 66 was one of the few major highways crossing the United States from east to west and is still identified by commemorative signs along sections where it has been preserved. Several years later, when the interstate system was built along the same route, the road was widened to four lanes, curves were straightened, and new bridges were built. The new highway was named Interstate 40.

On the east side of town was a small creek, a tributary to the Pecos River. Route 66 entered the valley through a long cut in the bluffs along the creek. The project called for widening the highway cut, widening the bridge over the creek, and then new pavement through the cut and on into town. We believed the job would be easy and fast construction. There was a stipulation in the contract that, during construction, Route 66 could not be blocked for more than one hour at a time.

The location was scenic. It was a nice place to spend the summer. Santa Rosa is in a semi-arid part of northeastern New Mexico. Scrub Pinion trees, Junipers, and Grease bush provide a pleasant scent which seems especially strong on hot, cloudless days.

Construction began in July, and tourist traffic at times was bumper to bumper. To widen the existing highway, it was necessary to blast the south side of the highway cut by several hundred feet and remove rock and earth as deep as 50 feet to allow for the additional widening.

Our expert in blasting was a fellow by the name of Johnson. Naturally, he was called "Swede." At that time, a road hand with dynamite-blasting ability was called a "powder monkey." Swede would stick out in a crowd, any crowd. He always wore a felt hat with a sweat-and dust-stained rim. Faded blue overalls with a rip in the seat was a trademark. He looked the part of a bar room fighter but was never seen in a bar; unusual for road hands.

Swede and I spent many hours carefully studying the area to be blasted. My faith and fate were in his hands. He had his early training working on new railroad construction during the 1920s in the western states. His education was of a practical "on-the-job" variety. Nevertheless, I never questioned his judgment. Swede convinced me he could set a series of delayed charges which would begin furthest from the highway cut. Then as the explosions occurred, each would be braced against the next blast a fraction of a second later; this would prevent debris from filling the roadway and would allow bulldozers and power shovels to quickly remove the blasted material. The highway then could be open for traffic within the specified one hour.

Swede worked two weeks drilling a series of deep holes and filling them with dynamite and delay blasting caps. The time arrived for the big blast. Highway engineers were notified and the state highway patrol advised to stop traffic. All were assured that backed-up traffic would be flowing again within an hour of the blast.

I parked my pickup on the opposite bluff above the creek. By two-way radio, I called Swede and told him to go ahead with the shot. He shouted "fire in the hole" and pushed the plunger down on the igniting battery box.

"Whomp!"

There was a muffled bang; and from my position, one-half mile away, I was surprised that the blast was not louder. The dust rose along the ridge to a great height. My first thought was that it looked like an atom bomb had exploded. A great cloud of dust lingered in the air, seemingly forever. I felt a lump form in my throat. Fear and uncertainty caused me to turn my head away from the sight. I couldn't bear to look. When the dust finally settled, I couldn't believe my eyes. The highway cut and the road through it had disappeared. The bluff across the way was level as though there had never been a highway entering Santa Rosa. My heart sank. I stared with disbelief. The inevitable consequences slowly unraveled in my thoughts.

Route 66 traffic had to be detoured south to the next bridge across the Pecos. This means the east and west traffic would require a 125-mile detour around Santa Rosa.

We worked steadily for three weeks clearing debris from the cut before the first traffic could pass. The roadway was rough for many days while equipment cleared boulders and earth from a narrow track through the cut. Equipment stopped working every other hour while the traffic slowly negotiated its way through the mess. Many cars scraped oil pans on rocks. Several oil pans and even fuel tanks were repaired or replaced. This did not necessarily bring an understanding smile from the car owners.

The project was completed as called for under the contract, however, a little later than originally planned. Swede would often explain that the rock was rotten and did not have solid mass to hold back the blast sequence. Fortunately, those were different and more-forgiving times. The company was not penalized for not fulfilling all of the conditions in the contract, and we were more-or-less forgiven by the highway patrol. I felt pity for the many summer tourists who were subjected to a hot, long detour around Santa Rosa.

Swede had another experience for his on-the-job training. I decided there must be a better way to earn a living, sold my share of the company, and went to South America, never forgetting that moment of a "sinking feeling."

The Peregrine Cricket

Paramaribo, Suriname, is about as close to tropical as you ever want to be. Temperatures usually hover around "just plain hot," but it gets a little hotter when it rains and the humidity shoots up. Still it's a very nice place to visit; located on the north edge of South America, Suriname attracted European colonists in the 1500s and 1600s.

Unlike much of the rest of South America, the Spanish did not choose to settle that part of the continent. Natives did not wear gold or silver jewelry; therefore, Spanish explorers correctly surmised there was no gold and no silver. They believed the sparse native population did not deserve Christian conversion, especially since they didn't have wealth to support new Spanish settlements made on behalf of the Spanish crown.

The Dutch were not so particular. They planted their flag on the spot which is now Paramaribo and called the colony, Dutch Guiana. (With independence from Holland, the name was changed to Suriname after the Suriname River, which runs through the country.) The Dutch were unaware at the time that their newly claimed territory would prove to have an abundance of bauxite. Bauxite looks like sticky clay in its natural state and is the mineral used to make aluminum.

Bauxite mines were the cause for me to visit Paramaribo during the mid 1960s. As a representative for a construction equipment manufacturer in Illinois, it was my job to visit the mine and listen to management complaints about our equipment performance. The equipment was used to excavate bauxite from the Billiton Mine.

Equipment complaints were usually detailed and lengthy. After a day or two of meetings, I would repack my suitcase and continue to the next stop, usually Caracas, Venezuela, for equipment discussions with a contractor who was building the Guri Dam on the Orinoco River in eastern Venezuela.

I had suitcase repacking down to a science. My pair of black business shoes were polished and kept in shoe socks to protect their shine, although I seldom had opportunity to wear them during my tour to various mine and construction sites. I spent most of the time in well-worn boots, which often had to be cleaned before entering hotel lobbies. My business suit was carefully packed, and it too went unused.

The last night in the hotel in Paramaribo, my sleep was interrupted constantly by the chirping of a cricket. The chirping was annoying; in fact, it was so annoying that I got out of bed more than once and searched the room to no avail for the persistent insect. I would happily have sent the little creature back to the tropics if I had found it. At least, that was my feeling earlier in the evening; by dawn, I would have crushed it with no remorse.

I made my way to the airport for an early-morning flight to Caracas. Not having slept the night before, I quickly fell asleep and landed at the Caracas International Airport at Maiquetia in what seemed like no time at all.

I resumed the routine of visiting a construction-site office and returning to the hotel for dinner and the night. Because I was exhausted, my suitcase was partially unpacked. I thankfully crawled into bed a bit earlier than usual and fell into a sound sleep. A short time later, I couldn't believe the noise. Suddenly, I was sitting upright in bed completely awake. It was a cricket chirping that caused it. It couldn't be! What had I ever done to crickets to deserve this? I was out of bed with purpose. This time I would find the "beast" and dispose of it.

I really didn't think I was being followed by crickets. This one had to be a Venezuelan cricket--surely not the same creature which had made my night so miserable in Paramaribo. Again, the chirping was loud and impossible to locate. I looked in every corner of the room, pulled open dresser drawers, looked at the closet shelves, searched through the bathroom towels, and even lifted the throw rugs and looked under them. Occasionally, the chirping would cease, and I would return to bed for mere moments before it was there again--chirp, chirp, chirp. The search process would resume.

Another night's sleep was disrupted, and I was off again to catch an early-morning flight. The next city on my tour was Bogota, Colombia. Again, I was able to sleep some on the plane but not enough to replace that lost the previous night. In Bogota, I met a business friend for lunch in the hotel dining room.

"You look awful!" was his greeting. "You must not be getting enough sleep!"

I welcomed the chance to tell the cause. After my story, his response was a loud laugh. "You are being followed by a peregrine cricket," he said with a big smile.

"What in the world is a peregrine cricket?" I asked.

"I just made that up. It means it's a wandering cricket."

It turned out that my friend was somewhat of an authority on crickets. "As I recall from high school biology class," he said with the aire of a professor, "a cricket is a member of the leaping orthopteran insect family. They are noted for ubiquitous chirping produced only by the males. They rub their forewings together to make the sound."

With a look of satisfaction, he continued: "I knew I would eventually be able to use that knowledge. I think I got an "A" on a test about insects like crickets."

"Hey, look!" I said, "There is no cricket alive, whatever his name, who could leap fast enough to keep up with a jet airplane!" We both laughed at that ridiculous idea.

After a full schedule of afternoon meetings, I again looked forward to an early and decent night's sleep. Convinced that the cricket problem was behind me in a Caracas hotel room, I unpacked my suitcase and climbed into bed. This time I had no chance to fall asleep. There was a cricket chirping loudly. I became panicky. This must be a conspiracy. I desperately needed sleep. Again, I systematically searched the room. A thought struck me. Perhaps the cricket was traveling with me in my suitcase! Whatever remained in the suitcase was emptied; everything was unpacked. I looked in pants pockets, shirt pockets, socks, and even inside the folds of three ties. Nothing. There was no cricket nor any other kind of bug.

The situation was not only becoming frustrating but bordered on complete idiocy. I gave up and went back to bed, again enduring a restless night's sleep interrupted by constant chirping.

The next morning, I was on a flight to Lima and to my room in the Hotel Bolivar. Exhausted from lack of sleep, I slowly unpacked my suitcase. Everything was put away with my suit hung in the closet. I took my shoes out of the protective socks, and suddenly, there it was--the Suriname cricket! It had been in my right shoe, trapped the whole time by the shoe sock.

The cricket looked at me as if to say, "You're tired? How do you think I feel? I've been calling for help over the last three days and nights!"

In spite of a cherished plan to crush the insect if I ever found it, I felt some pity for the creature. I gently picked it up. Cupped carefully in my hands, I took the elevator to the lobby and walked out a back door to the hotel flower garden. The cricket leapt from my hands and landed in a patch of forget-me-nots.

The Trouble
with Vinnitsa

Travel agents often know the best vacation spots and frequently learn of new places as a result of clientele seeking unusual and different travel destinations. Mary Beth Edwards was told not to be surprised by requests for odd airfares or hotel costs in strange locations. She had just opened Destinations Unlimited Travel, Inc., following a five-year apprenticeship with a large Omaha travel agency.

At first, she was unprepared for the type of customer encountered in the little town of Wheatfield. In Omaha, her usual job was routine computer searches for the cheapest airline flights to a variety of cities throughout the country. Most often, the requests were from a secretary making travel arrangements for her boss. Not so in Wheatfield. Since opening the agency, she found that the advice given her in Omaha was true. Most customers were retired farmers or ranchers. There were an occasional student from the Wheatfield Teachers College and very few businessmen.

It took Mary Beth a little while to understand the real interests of her special customers. The Ericksons were a typical example. She had met them during the first week she opened the agency in Wheatfield. They walked into her one-room office on Main Street while she was struggling to get the computer hooked up and tied into the travel industry.

"Hello, young lady. Welcome to Wheatfield. We're the Ericksons. We live just a couple of blocks away, over on Bluff. I'm John, but most of our friends call me Eric; and this is my wife, Elsa, and most of our friends call her Elsa." He made a laughing noise which sounded more like he was clearing his throat.

Elsa carried a bouquet of freshly cut flowers. "These are from our garden, dear. They are only in a Mason jar. Do you have some water?"

"Why, thank you very much. It is so thoughtful of you to welcome me to Wheatfield and bring flowers. They will brighten up this room. I haven't gotten around to hanging my travel posters and pictures yet. My name is Mary Beth Edwards, and I have an apartment on Pine Street off Cornfield Road. I really look forward to . . ."

John interrupted her before she could finish the sentence. "How old are you, Mary Beth?"

Elsa gave a sharp, disapproving glance toward John. "Oh, Eric, that's none of your business! Please excuse him, Miss Edwards. He's been in the sun and bumping along on a tractor too long. He has no manners!"

"That's all right. I don't mind, Mrs. Erickson." She turned and looked at John Erickson. "I'm 29 years old, went to school in Omaha, and worked for Universal World Travel there. That's where I learned the business, at least what I know about being a travel agent."

"You married?" John felt Elsa's elbow jab in his side.

"No, and I don't have a boy friend." Mary Beth couldn't prevent a slight blush and turned away with the jar of flowers in her hands. She walked to the small restroom at the back of the office; filled the jar with water, and returned to the metal desk, placing the flowers on the side away from the computer.

"Well, we're here to give you some business, young lady," Erickson said "and I might add, we're mighty glad you decided to open a travel office here. We've had to go all the way to Webster City to make travel arrangements, and that's 63 miles away."

John Erickson was over six feet tall. He appeared to be mostly bald under his John Deere cap. His short-sleeved shirt showed a deep tan but only to the elbows where bright, white skin took over. His face was heavily creased from exposure to all the seasons throughout the years. She guessed that the Ericksons were in their seventies. Elsa had stark, white hair which complemented her round face and apple cheeks.

"I'll be happy to help you. Are you planning a vacation?" Mary Beth sat at the desk and fidgeted with the computer mouse.

"Yes, we would like to take a trip; but we don't want to go to a Club Med. We've had enough Elderhostels and are not interested in anymore cruises. We want to do something unusual and go someplace where we haven't been before." Erickson pulled a straight-back chair close to the desk and sat down. Elsa moved toward the door and said she was going over to Walgreens and would be back in a few minutes. John took his billfold from his seat pocket, took out a newspaper clipping, and handed it to Mary Beth. "Take a look at this. We might be interested. Could you check it out? I'd like to know how much it costs. This doesn't give any information."

Mary Beth took the ragged-edged clipping and read aloud. "Experience the vacation of a lifetime aboard a real submarine. Space is limited. Call now for details. Submarine Vacations, Ltd." Hmm. Sounds unusual. There is no address. I think the phone number is for a place in Houston. I recognize the area code. Yes, I'll be happy to check on it for you. I'll find out what I can."

John got up and turned to leave. "Ma and me will come back tomorrow to see what you learned. Bye, Mary Beth. Good luck with your business. I think you're going to see a lot of folks like us. Nearly everybody around here is retired and looking for places to go--if only to get away from the kids and grandkids. Don't tell Mrs. Erickson I said that. She'd tear a strip off me. See you tomorrow."

Mary Beth said good-bye and picked up the receiver, listened for a dial tone, and dialed the number on the clipping. There were several rings. She was sure she would only get an answering machine. No business would let a phone ring so many times. She was right. The answering machine kicked in. "Hallo, you reach Submarine Vacations, Ltd. Please leave name and telephone number and date you call. We will respond you."

What a dumb message, she thought. What kind of an outfit is this anyway? The woman who made the taped message had a very strong accent. It might be Russian.

"Hello, this is Mary Beth Edwards, president of Destinations Unlimited Travel, Inc. I would like to receive information about submarine vacations as advertised." She gave the date and time of her call, phone, and fax numbers. "Please respond as soon as possible. Thank you."

John Erickson was at the travel office within minutes of Mary Beth opening the door. "Heard anything, Mary Beth?"

"Oh, good morning John. I mean Eric. No. Sorry. I called that number after you left yesterday but only got their answering machine. I asked that they call me back. Maybe I'll hear from them this morning."

"O.K., I'll check back with you later. Bye for now."

Two days passed. There had been no response. Mary Beth tried the Submarine Vacations' number several times but did not leave another message. John had dropped in several times asking if there was a reply. Each time he would make his visit a little longer. He seemed to enjoy recounting the Ericksons' previous travel experiences. She then understood why they were looking for something out of the ordinary. They had traveled everywhere: Europe, Asia, South America, and even to Nepal and Kilimanjaro.

On the third day, Mary Beth received a phone call from Submarine Vacations. It was a woman's voice, the same she had heard on the answering machine recording.

"Hallo, please. I wish speak to Edwards."

"This is Mary Beth Edwards; may I help you?"

"Here is Submarine Vacations, Ltd. You ask information. What your address? I send today."

Mary Beth decided there was little use in asking the woman for details over the phone. She slowly gave her name and mailing address, carefully spelling each word, and then repeating the entire address.

"Okay, I got. Spahseeba bolshoi. I send today. "Dah sveedahneeyah." There was a dial tone.

A week later, the Submarine Vacations' packet arrived. There were four sheets of paper: a cover letter and three forms. Mary Beth studied each page. The cover letter gave a brief description of documents.

She read aloud to herself.

"Dear Ms. Edwards. Enclosed, please find your application forms for a vacation of a lifetime. If accepted, you will board a nuclear submarine and spend five days and five nights aboard. Please note, each form must be completed in full before your application can be considered. Submarine Vacations cannot guarantee acceptance of your application. There is a limit to each boarding of only eight people. However, our next boarding has one vacancy, due to a cancellation. If you are interested, you must advise Submarine Vacations by telephone as soon as possible. However, based on the completed forms, we do reserve the right to refuse your application."

The second page was a typed form asking for a variety of details, including sex; marital status; age; submarine experience, if any; nationality; passport information; plus several questions which were of a probing and psychological nature, such as, "Do you have claustrophobia?"

The third form was very curious. Mary Beth read it over and over. She asked herself why they were making such conditions. She then studied the document, again, reading aloud,

"This agreement must be completed in its entirety, signed, and notarized. The applicant agrees unconditionally to the following:

1. I will not take pictures nor audio recordings at any time during the duration of the submarine

vacation.

2. Throughout the five days, I will use only my given name in any and all discussions with fellow vacationers. I will not divulge my family name, address, phone number, nor any other information which would allow anyone to open a dialogue or communicate with me in any manner following the conclusion of the submarine vacation.

3. I will not write about the submarine vacation in any form, including daily notes, personal diary, or letters describing the five-day vacation.

4. I will not discuss the submarine vacation with newspaper reporters or any member or agent of the media.

5. I will not discuss any details or offer information to any official of any government or any representative of any official agency sponsored by any government entity.

6. I will not hold Submarine Vacations liable for any misadventure, accident, bodily harm, illness, or any misrepresentations whether intended or implied."

There was a line for the signature of the client and a space for the notary's signature, date, and stamp.

"Good Lord, what in the world is this all about? I'm not sure I want any of my clients involved in this sort of thing."

She read the last page.

The cost of a five-day submarine vacation is $5,000. The cost includes all meals, alcoholic beverages, laundry, local transportation, and lodging. Not included is transportation to Cayenne, French Guiana, or the cost of visas, medical examinations, or health certificates. Special meal requests cannot be considered. The total of $5,000 must be made by certified check or bank transfer to the address below within ten days of notification of your application acceptance. None of the $5,000 will be refunded for any cause.

Submarine Vacations must receive the completed, signed, and notarized application forms within 14 days of the date shown in the cover letter.

Thank you for considering Submarine Vacations for your vacation of a lifetime.

Sincerely yours,
Anna Martinova
Vice President

"Wow! What an outfit. And what a price!" she said aloud. "John will hit the roof when he sees this."

Erickson appeared at his usual time. "Found out anything, Mary Beth?"

"Yes, it came this morning. You won't believe this." She handed Erickson the forms. "They are located in Houston. I thought so."

Erickson was silent as he studied each page. He pushed his John Deere cap back on his balding head, rubbed his open hand over his mouth, looked at Mary Beth, and said: "Hey, this might be just the thing we're looking for."

"It does sound different, doesn't it? I didn't think you would be interested. Actually, I wouldn't mind going on something like this myself. It sounds very exciting, doesn't it? A little expensive though." Mary Beth took the forms back from Erickson and looked at them again thoughtfully.

"Since you're a travel agent and all, they might give you a discount or even let you go free. Give them a call and see what they say."

"I don't really think I could leave my business-- especially not now when I'm just getting started. On the other hand, my sister did say she wanted to come see me. She might run the shop for five or six days. She's a more experienced travel agent than I am. O.K., I'll call them just to see what they say."

She picked up the phone and dialed the number of Submarine Vacations. "Hallo!" To her obvious surprise there was an answer and not the answering machine. She looked at Erickson and raised her eyebrows to indicate her surprise.

"Good afternoon. This is Mary Beth Edwards, president of Destinations Unlimited Travel, Inc., in Wheatfield. May I speak to Mrs. Anna Martinova, please?"

"Dah, here is Anna Martinova. You got your application forms, no?"

"Yes. They arrived this morning. I might have an interest in taking a submarine vacation. I see you have one space available. Since I am a travel agent, what discount would you allow?" She again looked at Erickson and smiled. After a moment she wrote $1,500 on a pad in front of her. "Oh, I'm afraid I couldn't afford that much. It would still cost $3,500."

Erickson held his right hand up, shaking it back and forth. "Excuse me, Mrs. Martinova. There is a person in my office who wants to speak to me." Mary Beth put her hand over the receiver and whispered to Erickson, "What is it?"

"Look, I'm willing to throw in $1,000. That will get you on the trip for half price, providing you give Ma and me a full account when you get back. That way, you'd know whether it would be safe enough for us to go and if it's worth it. My brother went down in a sub in the Pacific in '43. Since then, I've always wanted to take a trip in a sub to see what it's like. Go ahead, tell her you'll go. It's worth it to me to know whether it's O.K. for us to take the trip later."

Mary Beth hesitated while she stared at Erickson. He was serious. She hadn't really had a break for more than a year. "Mrs. Martinova, I'll send the forms to you by overnight delivery. I hope you accept my application."

"Another thing, Edwards. Do not bring suitcase. Just personal items, toothbrush, lingerie, rubber-soled sneakers. We furnish jumpsuits. No need dresses or blouse. I notify you by phone if accepted. You arrange transportation to Cayenne, French Guiana, and advise arrival time. We meet you."

Mary Beth quickly jotted down abbreviated notes and dates for arrival and departure from Cayenne. She asked several questions, but Martinova insisted Mary Beth would get answers to all her questions on arrival in French Guiana and hung up abruptly.

She put the receiver back in the cradle, looked at Erickson, and said: "I hope I'm doing the right thing. It's very generous of you to contribute $1,000. Are you sure you want to do that?"

"You bet I do. It'll be worth it for us. Like I said, it'll give us peace of mind if you say it's a worthwhile trip." He reached in his shirt pocket and took out a checkbook. "I'll write you a check for it now."

Two weeks later, Mary Beth was on a Caribe Air flight headed for Cayenne, French Guiana. The flight was over one hour late arriving. She was somewhat fearful no one would be there to meet her. That certainly would be a problem. She knew nothing of Cayenne and wouldn't know where to go. After immigration and customs procedures, she entered a hot and humid lobby. For a moment her fears were real. There was no one to meet her. It looked as though there were only the handful of passengers from her flight and families crowded around outside the terminal exit door.

From behind, she heard a familiar accent. "Mary Beth Edwards? Please come with me. You don't have luggage, no?'

"Yes, I'm Mary Beth Edwards. May I ask who you are?"

"Prahsteetyee. I mean, excuse please. I am Anna Martinova. We spoke on phone." She extended her hand to Mary Beth and smiled. Mary Beth was struck by Martinova's trim figure and petite size. She looked as though she could be a Russian ballerina and appeared to be about the same age as Mary Beth.

"I'm very happy to meet you, Anna. Thank you for meeting me."

"You're welcome. Come, there is car waiting. We go."

"Where are we going?" Mary Beth felt she was being rushed and wanted some time to get her bearings and ask some questions.

"We must hurry. We have to drive to town of Kourou north of Cayenne. We board launch there." Martinova led the way past the small gathering of women and children waiting for relatives or family members to claim their luggage. Above the shouted greetings, Mary Beth heard Martinova say to follow her to the end of the sidewalk in front of the terminal.

Parked on the road leaving the terminal was a black Peugeot. A young, tanned, blond-headed boy was standing with cap in hand, holding the rear passenger door open. He was neatly dressed in what looked to be a sailor's uniform with blue piping. He said, "Good evening, Miss Edwards. I am Pavel. I will be your driver to Kourou, and I will also operate the launch." Mary Beth was a little surprised by his accent-free American English. He had a distinctly foreign look about him; possibly the sailor's uniform was misleading. Mary Beth started to speak with a return greeting but was interrupted by Martinova.

"Enough, Pavel. You know we don't use last names. Remember that. Get in. Drive. Others waiting."

Martinova spoke with a cutting sharpness.

She got into the back seat next to Mary Beth. Bending over she whispered to Mary Beth, "Pavel my young brother."

That explains it, Mary Beth surmised. Older sister talk. "Where did he learn to speak English, Anna? He speaks like an American."

"Pavel live in Houston ten years. Graduate from University Houston. He's good boy."

"Are you married, Anna?"

"Yes. You will meet my man. He's chief of Submarine

Vacations. You will like him." Anna gave Mary Beth a smile.

Sunset was sudden. There was little light when they arrived at Kourou. A brief, but heavy tropical downpour caused a low mist to form, filtering what sunlight was left. The village streets were poorly lit.

The Peugeot slowly bounced its way down dirt streets filled with potholes. As they drove along the waterfront, Mary Beth could make out a thatched-roof hut, open on all sides, which seemed to serve as a waiting room. Alongside the hut was a rickety, wooden-plank dock where a canvas-topped launch was moored. Several people were seated on bamboo benches, out of the rain, under the thatched roof.

As Anna got out of the car, she said to Mary Beth, "We're here. Please come. Meet comrades who go with you."

Pavel was quick to walk down the dock and remove mooring ropes from the launch. The group of people in the thatched hut stood up and moved to the edge of the hut. Anna faced them and said, "Here is Mary Beth. She's last one. We go now. You introduce yourselves on launch. Please, everyone get in launch."

Mary Beth joined the group as they hurried down the shaky dock and boarded the launch, out of the rain. Pavel had the engine started and idling. As the last of the group boarded, he undid the remaining mooring rope and went back to the controls. The launch sped forward into darkness.

"Hi. I'm Curtis. This is my wife Eileen. Guess we can't use last names. You're Mary Beth, I believe Anna said." A heavy set, pleasant-looking man sat down next to Mary Beth.

"Yes, I'm Mary Beth." She extended her hand to Curtis

and then to Eileen. They looked to be in their mid fifties. "This is the most unusual vacation on which I've ever been. How about you all?"

Eileen answered, "Yes, it is for us as well. Our son, Elmer, is in the Navy. He's an officer in command of a submarine. He insisted we take this trip. The family took up a collection to pay for it. Expensive, isn't it? I think Elmer is more interested in finding out what it's all about--the secrecy and all. We've met everyone. Come, I'll introduce you."

"Sue Ann, meet Mary Beth. This is her husband, Bill." Sue Ann and Bill shook hands with Mary Beth. "Charles, Gene, John, meet Mary Beth." Each offered a firm handshake.

"Hello." Charles moved a step closer to Mary Beth.

"We're brothers. Two years between each of us. I'm the oldest, Gene is the youngest. People say we look the same age. We've even been told we look like triplets. I don't think so. I've been taking care of these two since they were born!" He laughed.

Gene and John chuckled and together said: "I don't think so. No way!" Mary Beth joined in the laughter.

Charles ignored the comments and continued, "We're all three firemen. Guess I can't tell you from where. Even though we look worn and old, I can tell you we're only in our thirties--just so you don't think we're as old as we look."

John quickly spoke up, "He's the oldest. Looks it, don't he?"

Mary Beth made some comforting comments about age and went back to her place near Curtis. "Everyone seems so nice. I think we'll have a good time together."

"Yes I agree." Eileen added.

The launch bounced along the swells. The smell of saltwater was strong. The heat and humidity were still uncomfortable in spite of the breeze from the speed of the launch. Rain continued to fall and pelted the canvas top. The group of nine fell silent, each lost in individual thought. About an hour past boarding, the launch motor returned to a near idle. In the darkness, the shape of a low hill could barely be seen on the starboard side.

Curtis broke the silence. "Looks like we're getting close to wherever we're going. We were told we'd have answers to our questions when we got to Cayenne. Haven't heard any yet."

Anna overheard the remark. "Everything will be clear. Be patient. Thank you."

The launch turned into the mouth of a river and continued at a slow speed. The smell of saltwater gave way to the musky odor of a tropical rain forest.

"It's so dark I can't make out the shoreline." Eileen commented.

Bill asked Anna: "Where are we? What's the name of this river? What's the name of the island?"

"Just a few minutes. The Captain and Mr. Ray will answer all questions."

The launch rounded a wide bend in the river. Mary Beth was the first to see the enormous shape in the darkness.

"Good Lord! Look! I had no idea a submarine could be so huge!" Everyone crowded to the starboard railing to see where Mary Beth was pointing.

In the darkness, the whale-like shape loomed out of the water. Each of the vacationers expressed amazement at the size. Sue Ann said, "It's so big, it's frightening." Her husband, Bill, simply repeated over and over, "My, my. Isn't that colossal? Isn't that colossal?" The rest of the group joined in with expressions of disbelief and descriptions of their impressions of the overwhelming size of the submarine.

As the launch approached the dock at the bow of the vessel, much of the surrounding shoreline was obliterated from view. There was a shroud of camouflage netting that covered the entire shape. Numerous ropes, cables, tubes, and wires extended from the submarine deck to the dock and beyond into the darkness. There were four or five bare lightbulbs hanging from a wire stretched from the dock to the submarine. The light was hardly strong enough to cast a shadow in the tropical downpour and mist rising from the mooring dock.

The launch bumped against the dock. A shadow materialized in the darkness. As he came close to the launch, Mary Beth could see it was a sailor, dressed in the same uniform as Pavel.

"Skaroh, quick!" Pavel called to the sailor as he threw the launch mooring rope to the sailor on the dock.

Anna turned to the gathering group. "Follow me quickly. Sorry, we have no umbrellas. Be careful not slip. Rain and oil make dock very slippery. Hurry!"

Eileen screamed, "I'm getting soaked!"

Sue Ann was a step behind her. "I can't see where I'm stepping! Hang on to me, Bill!" She called to her husband.

Pavel quickly jumped on the dock and held his hand out to Sue Ann. "Here, grab hold. Be careful of the ropes and cables. Watch where you step!"

Bunched closely together in single file, they followed Anna along the dock, walking fast, heads facing down. At the walkway from the dock to the submarine deck was a guard dressed in a black paramilitary uniform, holding a Kalishnikov automatic weapon at port arms. He was barely noticed in the darkness. Although rainwater flowed off his uniform, he did not seem disturbed by it and stood motionless as the column passed. By the time they entered through the submarine's deck hatch, everyone was soaked and dripping water. The ladies' hair was in shiny wet strings clinging to their foreheads. All except Anna. Obviously, she had known what to expect. She had a clear plastic rain hat covering her head.

Inside the submarine, the light was an eerie, dim red. There were hissing noises mixed with sharp metallic dings. Anna kept moving down a short ladder and through a narrow corridor with pipes, insulated cables, and tubes lining both sides. Each person stayed very close to the person directly in front of them, partly out of fear of being in such strange surroundings. Anna opened a steel door and walked through the hatch. The column of vacationers followed as they entered a wider corridor with doors on both sides. Each door had a brass number plate in the upper center.

Anna stopped, unfolded a sheet of paper, faced the group of eight, and called out: "Here quarters. I call name and tell assigned cabin number. Bill and Sue Ann, cabin ahdyeen ee tree; 'scuse, I mean one and three. You have door between cabins. Curtis and Eileen, two and four, connecting door. Mary Beth, five. John, six. Charles, seven. Gene, eight."

Anna stopped, unfolded a sheet of paper and continued with instructions. "In cabin, there are two blue jumpsuits. Please put one on. This is what you wear entire five days. Also, name tag. Please wear. If jumpsuit no fit, tell me, I get 'nother. Should all fit. We go by sizes you send on application. Also, same for sneakers. When you leave, cannot take sneakers or jumpsuits. Please, go to quarters. Dry off. Put on jumpsuits and meet in next compartment. It is passenger's lounge." She pointed toward the closed hatchway at the end of the corridor. "We meet together twenty-one hundred hours--nine o'clock. Thank you."

Thirty minutes later, Charles opened the hatch. The entire group had gathered behind him and followed, stepping over the hatch threshold into a spacious room which was well lit with several table lamps and fluorescent ceiling fixtures. One wall was lined with paperback and hard-cover books. Mary Beth glanced at the titles and realized there was a section of English books next to a row of German books, then Italian, Spanish, French, Russian, and Portuguese. In a corner of the room, was a pool table. Another corner had a VCR and television monitor. An opposite corner also had a VCR and monitor. Each had a shelf of videos, also in a variety of languages. There was a ping pong table, two exercycles, a Nordic exercise machine, and a treadmill.

John was the first to comment. "This is a submarine?"

Gene said, "Fantastic. Everything is here!"

Eileen remarked, "They must want us to stay in shape."

Anna appeared in the hatchway entrance. "Hey, look at this!" Charles was the first to notice her.

She was dressed in a starched, bright, white uniform with gold buttons, gold braid epaulets, and some sort of a red insignia on her right chest pocket. John thought she looked like a WAVE Admiral from World War II.

"Good. You look fine in jumpsuits. Everybody's fit O.K. You also follow orders good," she laughed. "You here on time. Please, find comfortable chair, sit. I hope quarters suitable. Captain and Mr. Ray will come soon now."

Mary Beth turned to Eileen, "I sure didn't expect to find such luxurious accommodations on a submarine--private shower and toilet, nice furniture, bedside reading lamp, good bed, better than home."

"Yes, it is surprising," Sue Ann joined in. The only thing that would make it better is a porthole, but I guess you can't have portholes in a submarine."

"Not hardly." Bill said.

Two men entered the passengers' lounge. The tallest was in a starched white officer's uniform with a gold braid lanyard and epaulets on each shoulder. There was a red insignia on his right jacket pocket, the same as Anna's. His cap had thick, gold braid on the peak. Silver gray hair showed beneath the cap and was neatly trimmed. He had a full, gray beard. Although showing a little age in the wrinkles of his tanned face, he could still pass for a distinguished, contemporary naval officer in any nation's navy.

Charles whispered to Mary Beth, "Man alive, that guy could pass for Sean Connery in the movie, 'Hunt for Red October.'" Mary Beth nodded her head in agreement.

The second man walked a few steps behind the uniformed

officer. As they entered the center of the lobby, he stepped ahead and stopped before the seated passengers. He looked younger than the officer and a couple of inches shorter. Mary Beth thought he must be in his late forties, looking trim and athletic, dressed casually in a print shirt and tropical-weight, light-tan slacks. He was the first to speak.

"Welcome, Ladies and Gentlemen, to Submarine Vacations. I know you all will have a memorable time. My name is Peter Ray. I am an American. I am also president of Submarine Vacations, Ltd."

Mary Beth glanced at Anna. Anna returned a pleasant grin. So this is Anna's husband, Mary Beth thought. Anna must have kept her maiden name.

Ray continued the briefing. "You will be on board this vessel for the next five days. The entire staff on board also welcomes you and will do everything possible to ensure that you have a pleasant time with us. I know you have many questions, but first I would like to introduce the people with whom you will have the most contact." He looked to the corridor. Pavel had entered the lounge. "You have already met Seaman Pavel. You have also met Lieutenant Anna, who also happens to be my wife, Mrs. Ray."

There was a murmur of surprise. Curtis said softly, with an expression of disbelief, "'Also happens to be my wife!'"

"You undoubtedly have wondered why we have insisted on using first names only. It is a matter of great importance that security is maintained during our five days together and that same security be continued after you leave us. Obviously, if you do not know the full names of your fellow passengers, you will not be in contact with them following our time together. It may seem harsh and unfair, but I believe you will understand the need for such security upon completion of your stay with us. The only complete names you will know are mine, Lieutenant Anna's, and that of our captain. May I now introduce the commander of this submarine, Captain Yury Martinov." The American stepped back to stand at the side of Anna. Martinov took a step forward toward the seated passengers.

"Welcome aboard the SSQ Vinnitsa. This is a Delta I Class Nuclear Submarine built in the Soviet Union in 1972. This vessel was originally built as a strategic missile cruiser and was assigned to the Northern Fleet which has its headquarters in Severomorsk. It was named after the village of Vinnitsa in the Ukraine near Kiev. In 1985 the Vinnitsa was re-designated as a communications relay vessel, which it remains today. A few years ago, this submarine was sold to others. It is no longer owned nor operated by the Russian Navy. This is not an unusual occurrence. Over the past 50 years, Russia has exported 150 submarines. I am not at liberty to identify the new owners of the Vinnitsa."

Martinov looked directly at each of the passengers. The brief silence intensified attention. He spoke slowly with comfortable authority. He was obviously Russian, but his accent was cultured British English. Charles again whispered in Mary Beth's ear, "He even talks like Sean Connery."

He continued. "Measurements and dimension are normally given in meters; however, I will translate these into feet. The Vinnitsa is 469.3 feet long, 38.4 feet wide, and 28.2 feet high. We have nearly 18,000 square feet of interior deck."

Bill shook his head and said, "This is a big boat. Really big."

"Fully submerged, we displace over 10,000 tons."

"What's that mean?" Eileen quietly asked. Her question went unanswered.

"This vessel is powered by steam turbines and has a cruising speed of 25 knots. There is no armament of any type on board. No torpedoes, no missiles. In fact all of the missile silos have been removed. This room, your cabins, dining room, and passengers' galley are located in the section where missile silos once stood."

The passengers looked at one another in wonder. Curtis remarked aloud, "I wondered how there could be such a large room on a submarine. That explains it."

"During your five days aboard the Vinnitsa, you will hear a multitude of strange sounds. Permit me a few minutes to explain the workings of a submarine.

"A submarine is fundamentally an airspace contained by a hull that is designed to withstand deep ocean pressures and to move easily underwater. The hull is a double steel shell. The inner, or pressure, hull contains the machinery for propelling and guiding the vessel, plus living quarters and a variety of equipment, depending on the assigned task given the submarine. In the case of the Vinnitsa, we have a great deal of high-tech communication equipment, which I am unable to discuss due to the secret nature of our operation." Martinov walked to the wet bar and filled a glass with water. He took a sip and continued his lecture.

"The outer hull holds the ballast tanks. When the vessel submerges, these tanks are opened and flooded with seawater. For surfacing, the seawater is forced out of the ballast tanks and replaced by compressed air. Flooding the ballast tanks is only one step in the process of submerging. The submarine is also propelled downward by rear-mounted propellers that force the craft forward and by diving planes, which are movable horizontal rudders that direct the angle of the dive. When the desired depth is reached, the water level in the vessel's trim tanks is adjusted to keep the craft stable."

He took another sip of water, again looked at each passenger, and said, "You will hear many noises when any of these functions occur. Do not be concerned; they are normal. Tomorrow morning, we will have escape instructions. This is only a precaution in case of an emergency. Think of the procedure as the same as escape instruction given on commercial airlines. It is nothing more.

"You will have noticed the conning tower as you entered the vessel. On nuclear submarines, the conning tower is known as the 'sail' and carries a set of diving planes. The sail also holds the periscope, certain radio and radar antennas, and the snorkel, which is a system of air intake and exhaust pipes."

Martinov eased into an overstuffed leather lounge chair. He extended open hands toward the group and said, "Now, any questions before we proceed to the dining room for an evening snack?" He looked at a wall clock. "Shto, what! It's after ten o'clock. This will be a late-night snack. I'm afraid I have kept you far too long."

"Captain," Charles spoke first, "Where did you learn to speak such good English?"

"Ah, I'm not so sure I do. But, I spent many years in England. I received a degree from Oxford University. I also have read every book Zane Grey has written. You will notice the library has several Zane Grey books." He pointed to the bookcases along one wall.

Bill spoke up, "How deep will we be going?"

"Not very deep. Much of the time, we will be at periscope depth." Martinov replied. "You will have opportunities to enter the sail and look through the periscope. I will announce over the speaker system if there is anything worthwhile seeing. Due to the nature of our mission, we will not surface during the entire five days. We have the ability to be submerged much longer than five days. We will also avoid raising the periscope during daylight in order to avoid detection."

Sue Ann asked, "How many crew are on board?"

Martinov replied, "This submarine originally required a crew of 110. Without armament and without missiles, we have a very scaled-down compliment. You will not see the crew during our voyage. They will be in the bow area and in the engine room. The exact number of crew is classified for security considerations."

"Mr. Ray, how often do you offer submarine vacations? Why do the owners allow passengers on their submarine?" Curtis was standing with a hand resting on the back of Eileen's chair.

"We have sailings three or four times a month; they are always limited to eight passengers. The owners of this vessel wish to keep it operational as long as possible. They are not wealthy. In fact, hard currency is difficult for them to come by. Therefore, as a means of defraying a little of the tremendous costs of operation, they decided to offer space to passengers."

Mary Beth asked Martinov, "What's the need for such secrecy?"

Martinov answered, "The owners purchased the Vinnitsa for certain intelligence gathering. They do not want the world to know their activities. You no doubt noticed the camouflaged netting covering the submarine. This is a small, obscure, and uninhabited island in the Iles du Salut chain, owned by French Guiana. The infamous Devil's Island is not many kilometers from here. The government has given the owners permission to dock the Vinnitsa at this location."

Gene stood up and said, "Where is this snack you suggested?'

Ray answered, "Follow me. I'm a bit hungry myself." He led the way to a door at the far end of the lounge. In single file, the passengers entered a well-furnished dining room where the tables were covered with starched, white tablecloths. On each of the half-dozen tables, freshly cut flowers in silver vases were placed along with bottles of French wine. At each place setting was a printed menu.

The chef stood by the galley door. Martinov pointed to the neatly dressed cook and said, "Here is the culprit to blame if you leave with more pounds than you came. Please meet Pierre, the best chef this side of Paris." Pierre smiled widely, made a slight bow, turned, and entered the galley.

Following the light supper, Ray announced, "Please return to the passengers' lounge or your cabins. We will be underway within a few minutes."

Back in her cabin, Mary Beth took a small notebook from her tote bag. She said to herself, "I'm going to keep a diary of this trip, regardless of the secrecy agreement. I must have some details to tell the Ericksons. After all, Eric paid $1,000 for me to be here." She began jotting down notes of the happenings since landing in Cayenne. Suddenly, there were numerous noises and vibrations. The Vinnitsa was underway.

The compartments were comfortably air conditioned. The passengers slept well. There was no sensation of the submarine's movement, only slight vibrations along with steady humming and hissing which resembled comforting background music.

Following breakfast, the passengers gathered in the lounge. Curtis, Eileen, Bill, and Sue Ann were quick to start a bridge game. Charles and Gene were playing pool, and John challenged Mary Beth to ping pong. By midday, the VCR was on. Mary Beth and the three brothers were watching "Sleepless in Seattle."

Charles remarked, "Guess what? I see they have 'Hunt for Red October.' Want to watch that after lunch? It's really an appropriate movie for the occasion. Better than 'The Towering Inferno.' That's also there, but it's too close to home. We're trying to forget work."

After lunch, the VCR movies were forgotten. The three brothers went to their compartments for naps; the two married couples were back at their bridge game; and Mary Beth was engrossed in a novel.

"Now hear this! Now hear this!" The announcement shattered the tranquillity of the lounge and awoke the brothers from their napping. The vacationers instantly became attentive.

The announcement continued, "This is your captain speaking. The Vinnitsa will now undergo silent running. All hands and passengers remain silent and avoid knocking or scraping noises. We have detected a submarine hunter in the area. That is all." The announcement was then repeated in Russian.

Eileen looked concerned. She spoke in a whisper to the other three seated at the bridge table. "I'm frightened. What's it mean? Will they drop depth charges and sink us? I wish we hadn't come."

"No, nobody's going to sink us," Curtis said in an effort to comfort his wife. "There isn't a war on. I think the captain simply doesn't want that ship to know we're here."

Bill added, "I think you're right, Curtis. There's no need to worry."

Mary Beth quietly left the lounge and returned to her compartment, carefully closing the door trying not to make a sound. She sat down at the small writing desk and wrote in her notebook: "First day out. Captain has announced that there is a sub hunter in the vicinity. We're on silent running." It was the first she noticed that the vibrations, humming, and hissing had stopped.

Twenty minutes later the captain was again heard over the speaker system. "Now hear this! Now hear this! Resume activities. That is all." Vibrations, humming, and hissing noises began again.

After the first announcement, the bridge players stopped the game and simply looked blankly at one another, each trying to conceal their concern. After the all-clear announcement, Bill remarked, "Well, that was exciting, wasn't it?" The bridge game resumed.

Four days passed. Mary Beth kept the activities and incidents noted. "There have been several silent runnings over the past four days. Sometimes it seems we have stopped moving for no reason. We have been able to visit the sail in the evenings and observe operating activities in the control room. There are only two crewmen in the control room. They never speak. The captain has allowed us to look through the periscope several times. He calls to one of the crewmen in the sail and shouts, 'Up

periscope!' bends down and rises with the periscope as it ele-
vates. Most of the time it is difficult for us to make out anything.

"The second night out the Captain pointed out the lights
of Georgetown, Guiana. We have also observed ships. One was
lit up like a Christmas tree. The Captain said it was a Holland
Line cruise ship. We have also looked at the lights of Port of
Spain, Trinidad. Last night, we were able to view Grenada from
a stationary position. It seems this is the objective of the
Vinnitsa. Why, no one has been able to guess.

"The Captain, Mr. Ray, and Anna eat every meal with us.
They have answered many operational questions but avoid
answering anything pertaining to the objective of the voyage or
any ownership questions.

"Pavel serves as our steward. He cleans the
compartments, makes the beds, and also serves at mealtimes. He
has not been as talkative as when we first met him. He hardly
says a word when the captain, Anna, or Mr. Ray are present.

"Everyone seems very content. The three brothers spend
time on the exercise machines, watch VCR movies, and play
pool. The two married couples play a lot of cards and have been
reading books from the lounge library. I have also been reading
quite a bit. The meals have been excellent, as good as any
five-star restaurant. The open bar is very nice as well.

"Tomorrow will be our fifth day out. We will disembark
tomorrow night. So far, the experience has been highly unusual.
I notice my fellow passengers are quietly exchanging full names
and home towns. I believe the three firemen brothers are from
Cleveland; Curtis and Eileen are from Albuquerque; Bill and Sue
Ann are from Denver.

"From the looks of the various language books and

movies, Submarine Vacations must cater to many foreign passengers. On this voyage, it appears they accepted only Americans."

At dinner on the fifth night, the passengers were chatting with one another on a most familiar, friendly basis. Being together for five days had created a comradeship. It seemed everyone had enjoyed the experience. Mary Beth was talking to Eileen about the way everyone was compatible and friendly, even with an open bar. She remarked how difficult it could have been if there was animosity for any reason. She was about to make a final point when Pavel bent over her left side and placed a dinner plate in front of her. She looked to his feet as she made room and was surprised to notice mud on his shoes. She made no comment about it.

After dinner and a short time in the lounge sipping an after-dinner drink, Mary Beth went to her compartment. Something wasn't right. How did Pavel get mud on his shoes? It was fresh. She couldn't think of a logical reason. She listened to the steady humming and hissing. Something is very wrong, she thought.

At two o'clock, she still hadn't been able to get to sleep. She dressed in the jumpsuit and went to the lounge. No one was there. She then walked down the dimly lit corridor toward the sail, hoping the captain might be there. The light in the control room had a red hue. There was no one to be seen. She walked down a narrow, dark passageway to a partially closed door marked "Entry Prohibited" in English. Beneath that, was: "Danger, Peligro, Ahpahsnah, Verboten," all in red lettering.

The door was slightly open. Mary Beth peered in through the opening. She could make out a stack of audio tape decks. She smelled cigarette smoke which was surprising since it had been strongly emphasized in one of the briefings there was to be no smoking on board. She moved the door silently and could see a crewman sitting with his back to her. Unbelievably, he was watching live TV not a tape. It was a newscast. She could see the station identification on the screen: "TV French Guiana."

Mary Beth returned to her compartment. No one had seen her. She lay awake until early morning before finally falling asleep. At breakfast, she did not join in the group conversations. She was puzzled. Something was wrong.

The day went quickly. Ray and the captain joined the group in the lounge shortly after they were told the Vinnitsa had docked. A short talk was given by the captain. He recounted the route of the voyage and again asked that all participants honor the secrecy agreement they had signed. Ray thanked the group for taking a vacation with Submarine Vacations and hoped that it had been all they expected. Each of the group, except Mary Beth, also expressed their thanks and appreciation to the captain and Mr. Ray.

They left the Vinnitsa in single file just as they had arrived five days earlier. It was still raining. Mary Beth did not join the group. She stopped and looked at Ray with purpose.

"I want to talk to you. There are some things that need explaining." She described her activities the night before and also spoke of the fresh mud she saw on Pavel's shoes.

Anna was on the dock in the rain. She called back to Mary Beth. "Please come, everyone in the launch. We're waiting you."

Ray answered, "Go ahead without Mary Beth, Anna. I will bring her later in the supply boat."

"Are you sure? We can wait few minutes." Anna shrugged.

"Yes, I'm sure. Shove off, Anna." Ray turned to Mary Beth and led her back into the submarine. They went to the lounge. He turned to her and asked if she would like a drink. "No thank you," she replied. Ray poured Scotch into a glass and took a quick sip.

"Mary Beth, I am going to tell you the complete story about the Vinnitsa, and I will do so with the hope you will understand and act accordingly."

"Try me," she responded.

"This is going to take some time. I want you to appreciate all the factors and circumstances surrounding this vessel and our activities." He took another sip of Scotch.

"You may not recall or perhaps never heard of the incident; however, in early October, 1986, a Russian yankee class ballistic missile submarine, designated K219, had an accidental explosion in a missile tube. It was adrift in the Atlantic for several days and finally sank 600 miles from Bermuda on October 6, 1986. Many ships and submarines of the Russian Northern Fleet were sent to assist K219. Most arrived too late. About half the crew was lost.

One of the Fleet's submarines sent to assist was the SSQ Vinnitsa under the command of Captain Martinov. The Vinnitsa was within 150 nautical miles of K219 when she developed problems with submerging equipment. This was at a time when the Russian military was suffering funding problems, and the navy neglected proper fleet maintenance.

"Normally, the equipment failures wouldn't have been a serious problem, but a strong hurricane had been tracked heading directly for the location of the Vinnitsa. Captain Martinov was ordered by Northern Fleet headquarters at Severomorsk to sail the Vinnitsa west toward the northeast coast of South America to avoid being overtaken by the hurricane.

"The Vinnitsa continued west, but by the time it reached the Iles du Salut group of islands, it was overtaken by the hurricane. Martinov sought refuge in a river inlet; this river where we are now. When the hurricane passed, the Vinnitsa was trapped in silt deposited by flooding from the hurricane. In fact, the entire river had been heavily choked with silt. The vessel was helpless.

"Over a six-month period, a variety of tugs and repair ships from the Northern Fleet tried unsuccessfully to move the Vinnitsa. Extensive dredging was carried out, but the submarine was too deeply sunk into the mud. Every effort failed to free the vessel. Finally, the decision was made to strip the submarine. All reusable machinery, equipment, and instruments were removed. What wasn't reusable was taken to deep water and dumped. After the stripping project was completed, Captain Martinov was reassigned to the Russian Navy's Scrap Yard Office in Moscow."

Mary Beth began to ask a question. Ray raised his hand and said, "Please, let me tell you the entire story first."

"At the time, I worked for a tug and salvage company out of Antwerp. I was in charge of their Houston office. One of my projects was to secure scrapped vessels from the Russian Navy. We sold scrap ships to China. My contact within the Russian Navy was Captain Martinov. We became very good friends. He introduced me to his family: his son, Pavel, and his daughter, Anna, whom I later married."

Ray took another sip of Scotch and said to Mary Beth, "Sure I can't fix you a drink?"

"No, thank you. Please continue. I'm not sure where this

is leading."

"Thank you for your patience. I'm about to conclude the story. Martinov told me about the Vinnitsa stuck in the mud off French Guiana. It had been designated for salvage. One evening, while we were having a drink in the Metropole Hotel in Moscow, he told me the complete story of the Vinnitsa. He said he hated to think of the submarine being scrapped. He had a plan and wanted my advice and assistance.

"He suggested that my company could buy the salvage rights but not scrap the vessel immediately. Rather, we could turn it into a tourist attraction. The Antwerp company actually bought the idea and gave us a year to show profit. To make a long story short, we came up with a plan to fix up living quarters, put some obsolete instruments back in the sail, and wire the passenger area with concealed speakers. Martinov was able to get sound tracks of submarine noises from a Moscow movie company. We made a machine that would create vibrations in the hull.

"The electrical power is provided by a diesel generator on shore, away from the docks. It's Pavel's responsibility to maintain the generator. He frequently left the submarine to attend to the unit. He has been told to change shoes before re-entering the passenger's area. He didn't do it. That's why you saw fresh mud on his sneakers.

"After we set the project up with my company, Martinov resigned from the Russian Navy. Anna and I were living in Houston. Pavel had joined us earlier and was going to school there. We contracted out the refurbishing to a Belgian company associated with the salvage company I worked for. Within a year we were in business.

"We advertised submarine vacations in Europe and Asia and only recently in the United States. For each 'voyage,' we kept reservations limited to eight people and always from the same country. We have been in operation for five years. Our gross income has been almost two million dollars a year. We pay a percentage to the government of French Guiana. Overhead is low. The captain recruited people from Russia to maintain the appearance of the submarine. That camouflage netting covers up an awful lot of rust and ugliness. Seeing the submarine only in the darkness also helps. So, that's the story."

"I can't believe it!" Mary Beth had a shocked expression. "How could you do it? You are all frauds. You should be reported for deceiving people."

"Yes, I can understand your outrage, Mary Beth. But look at it this way. Is it any different than what happens at Disneyland? People go there and are entertained with the same sort of make-believe. We do much what they do. If people knew that the Vinnitsa was mired down in deep mud and couldn't move if it had to, would they show any interest? As it is, our guests leave here with a feeling they have had the experience of a lifetime and memories which would be impossible to come by under any other circumstances. And I might add, this occurs under very safe and comfortable conditions."

"It's still very deceitful. What about the lights we saw in the periscope?"

"Oh, I guess that is also a little deceitful. We have clear Christmas tree lights strung up at various spots and distances. That's what you saw. That's also why we only raise the periscope in the dark."

Mary Beth shook her head. She became flush with rage. "I'm shocked. Really shocked. Everyone has been duped. Now I know why you want everything kept a secret. You don't want people to check on you. What about that armed guard in black?

The man with a rifle we saw when we boarded the submarine? What's that all about?"

Ray stood up and put his empty glass back on the bar. "That fellow is a local guy from Cayenne. The automatic rifle is a stage prop. I doubt he has ever had a real rifle in his hands.

"Well, that's the story. What do you plan to do with it? We only have a couple of years left and then the Vinnitsa will have to be scraped. The bottom is rusting out, and Antwerp wants to salvage the metal before it's of no value."

"I really don't know what I am going to do with your revelations. I just don't know. Will you take me back to shore now? I have a plane to catch."

On the flight from Cayenne, Mary Beth went over and over the strange events. What was she going to tell the Ericksons? She felt a fool for falling for such a hoax.

The next day, both the Ericksons were at the travel office within minutes of Mary Beth opening the door.

"How did it go, Mary Beth?" Erickson asked. "Was it safe? Was it a real adventure?" He pushed his John Deere cap back on his head.

Ella added, "What do you recommend, Mary Beth? Should we go or do you think it is too dangerous?"

Mary Beth hesitated, then smiled, and said, "It's no more dangerous than going to Disneyland. You'll have a real good time."

Five Days in
La Paz

La Paz, Bolivia, has four seasons--everyday. Early morning is like spring; by 10:00 A.M., it begins to feel like summer; and at 3:00 P.M., there is autumn in the air. Winter comes as the sun sinks behind the Andes mountains to the west. Take a stroll at noon in short sleeves; and if you don't have a sweater or jacket, you will be looking for a coffee shop by 3:30 in the afternoon. Actually, hot chocolate is equally popular at that time of day. Visitors to La Paz often find it difficult to adapt to both the lack of oxygen and the sudden cold in the afternoon and evenings.

La Paz is nestled in a wide canyon at a 12,500-foot elevation. It is on the east side of the Andes with 20,000-foot peaks and higher only a short distance away. The commercial airport is on a 14,000-foot plateau twenty miles or so west and up the canyon from La Paz.

In spite of altitude and lack of oxygen, I enjoyed my visits to La Paz. It wasn't a long flight from Lima on the Peruvian coast, where I resided at the time. I was there as the Latin American representative for a construction and mining equipment manufacturing company located in Illinois. Even though I regularly visited the major cities in Latin America for business purposes, I liked to visit La Paz the most. Why, I can't adequately explain. Friends and business acquaintances would look at me with wonder when I would mention my favorable feelings about La Paz. For the most part, they would avoid trips to Bolivia whenever possible and would travel there only when business circumstances were such that they could not provide an acceptable excuse to avoid the trip. Even then, they would make sure that the visit was for minimum amount of time. After several trips to the city, I made a variety of friendships and usually looked forward to my flights to La Paz.

The only acceptable means of reaching Bolivia from anywhere was by plane. No doubt some locals who could not afford a plane ticket would find other means, such as a slow, crowded train or a rickety antique bus or even walking or traveling by horse and cart; but very few visitors would consider anything but airline travel. Travel by bus is considered the least desirable. There were frequently reports of busses going off the roads and crashing down the mountainsides, killing many or all on board.

La Paz is the capitol of Bolivia. It may never have come into existence if it weren't for the tin mine, and perhaps the capitol would now be at a more friendly elevation and comfortable climate in the tropical area of Bolivia to the east. However, Spanish conquistadors were looking for gold and silver, and tin was as close as they could come to it in Bolivia, and the tin was on a 14,000-foot plateau. That elevation was too much for the Spanish invaders, so they went 2,000 feet down the canyon and built a settlement which has survived as the center of commerce and industry for the country as well as the political base. High altitude is known to change personalities, usually for the worse. The brain becomes starved for oxygen, and that fact may explain why Bolivia is noted for explosive revolutions, revolutions which usually begin with unhappy laborers in the tin mines on the 14,000-foot plateau.

During the mid-1960s, I visited La Paz every couple of months. Usually, my visits were uneventful but enjoyable. On one visit, I had the opportunity to spend a weekend skiing on the Chaclataya Glacier. The ski area was primitive. There was one short rope tow. It was at 17,000 feet, and no one skied very long. I spent much of the time in a cabin with an oxygen bottle. My one experience was sufficient.

My last visit to La Paz lasted five days, and those five days have lasted in my memory as well. Although I was always aware of the political circumstances in all South American countries, since political change would usually affect business, I was never too concerned with the causes resulting in new political control. Thus, in spite of hearing of the unrest in the Bolivian tin mines, I didn't hesitate to arrange a regular visit to La Paz. The government had recently purchased a quantity of road construction equipment, and my factory was always interested in government officials' comments, especially if they indicated that they would be placing more orders.

I sent a cable to Señor Hugo Velasco, the dealer in La Paz, to arrange meetings with the appropriate officials and to book me into the La Paz Crillon Hotel. Hugo was well educated and spoke excellent English. His family was considered Spanish-European, a group which represents about 8 or 10 percent of the six million population and holds most of the wealth. Indians account for 55 percent, and Mestizos (Indian-Spanish mixtures) make up the balance of the population.

For the most part, the Indian-Spanish population was often restless, especially the miners. The Indian population still consists of two basic groups: those living in the Andes, who are descendants of the Incas, and those living in the tropical rain forest on the east side of the country at much lower altitudes. Both groups generally stay within their cultural habitats with the exception of some young and ambitious men and women from the rain forest and from Andean villages who migrate to the cities, especially La Paz, to seek work which is usually poorly paid and menial. They often join the masses of the restless. During the time of this story and originating in the early 1950s with the nationalization of the tin mines, universal suffrage, and redistribution of land to the Indians, the political conditions changed frequently.

Following most periods of unrest, the military seized control. Over a brief 30-year period, there have been nearly 200 coups. With such frequency of riots, coups, and military intervention, most travelers to Bolivia ignored warnings and with reason. The unrest generally was kept from the center of La Paz so that foreigners and businessmen were usually unaware of the happenings. However, on this occasion, visitors to La Paz would have been well-advised to heed the warnings.

I arrived in La Paz and was met by Hugo, who took me to the Crillon Hotel. A full day of meetings had been arranged for the next day. After a troubled night trying to adjust to sleeping at over 12,000 feet, I was met by Hugo at 8:00 in the morning to begin our round of meetings. Hugo expressed some concern about the miners' unrest, saying that the riots were a bit more widespread than usual and could possibly get out of control. I don't think I fully understood, nor listened, to his concern. My thoughts were on the various meetings I would be having during the next few days. I had to be prepared to answer a variety of questions and complaints concerning the performance of the equipment recently purchased by the government. I could anticipate questions that would have to be referred to the factory for adequate answers, and that always made officials upset, believing that no answers would be forthcoming. As it happened, they were often right.

Our first meeting was at 8:30 A.M. We arrived promptly and were ushered into a waiting room to sit for thirty minutes while the Deputy Director for road equipment drank coffee and killed time in his office until satisfied we would be sufficiently grateful to see him and would graciously accept his apology for the delay.

His name was Jose Blanco, obviously a political appointee. This was always apparent in previous meetings. He really didn't know a grader from a dump truck. Nevertheless, he was a pleasant fellow to talk to, and he always offered coffee or hot chocolate and cookies. Appointments with him were not a total waste, and they were necessary since he would suggest we visit with his subordinate, the equipment supervisor, and the person who actually knows the equipment, problems, and applications. He would officiously phone the engineering department and ask for Engineer Crespo, this done with a deeper than normal voice. He would then advise Crespo that the equipment people would be visiting him shortly.

On our way to Crespo's office, we passed the square in front of the government office complex where the president's office was located. Hugo would point out the lamppost on the plaza where a recently deposed president had been hanged by a mob. Hugo seldom failed to point it out whenever we passed the plaza. This was often since the main street through La Paz went past it. Other points of interest never rated quite as much attention.

When we reached Engineer Crespo's office building, there was obvious excitement and commotion in the air. Taxis and trucks and passenger cars, accompanied by urgent horn blasts, seemed to move faster and more erratically than usual.

Crespo met us in the building lobby and escorted us up the ancient elevator to his office on the top floor. Crespo was an efficient bureaucrat. I noticed he had an open notebook on his desk, which I correctly assumed contained the points he would bring up during our meeting. Shortly into our discussions, there was the sound of aircraft performing aerobatics; but it was no air show. Crespo casually turned toward the window, and said, "They're strafing the miners."

This matter-of-fact statement raised Hugo's eyebrows and sent a shiver down my spine. I got up and went to the window; but as someone once remarked, you only see dirty windows, never clean ones. Crespo's office windows were almost opaque. It was likely the windows had not been touched since the day they were installed, probably fifty years before. Crespo suggested we go up to the roof for a better view. We did but could only see two ancient biplanes performing low-level maneuvers. If they were strafing, they were too far away for us to hear machine-gun fire.

We returned to Crespo's office and finished our meeting with no further discussion concerning the riots or revolution, if in fact that is what it was turning into. Hugo took me back to the Crillon Hotel and suggested that I stay in my room. He told me he would be back in the morning at the same time to make our other appointments. That plan was wishful thinking. It was not to happen.

.　　A message was handed me with my room key. The U.S. Embassy Deputy Chief of Mission had called to invite me to dinner at his residence that evening. I had spent some time with him, and he seemed always eager to talk with American business people, not necessarily about business. He and his wife liked to talk generally about their life stateside and how they looked forward to returning after their tour in Bolivia. That attitude was not uncommon among embassy personnel wherever. Nevertheless, I welcomed the chance to have a home-cooked meal. I left the hotel on foot since the deputy chief's residence was close enough to the hotel. Walking was generally a better choice than taking a taxi which, for the most part, would likely have some unidentifiable odors and possibly pieces of seat springs sticking out of the upholstery.

I left the hotel without a sweater, which later proved an error. The streets were deserted for early evening. This was unusual but understandable considering the earlier happenings. A taxi roared by at great speed with its horn blaring. Out of the back-door window, two legs hung limply--a wounded miner being rushed to the hospital was my guess. The trouble was not over.

By the time we were seated at the DCM's table for dinner, I was feeling a chill and occasionally coughing. The dining room was cold. If there were any homes, offices, or stores in La Paz with central heating or any kind of heating, I never found them. The embassy at least had supplied the DCM with a small electric heater. Following dinner, I stood as close as I could to the heater and tried to warm up to little avail. The DCM warned that pneumonia comes fast at the La Paz altitude, and I should take care. As I was about to leave, he received a message from the embassy that martial law had been declared in La Paz. He advised that I return to the hotel as quickly as possible, lamenting that he did not have a car available to take me.

The streets were dark and completely deserted on my return walk, which was more like a jog. I was still in shirt sleeves and very cold. It was about 10:00 P.M. when I got to my room. My coughing was constant. Breathing was becoming difficult. After a hot bath, I piled on the blankets and fell into a half sleep. By 1:00 A.M., I was fully awake and gasping for air between coughs. I phoned the desk and asked that a doctor be called to my room.

The desk clerk said: "Impossible. There is not a chance. There is a martial law curfew! No one is allowed on the streets. You could be shot by soldiers."

I tried to go back to sleep. That was impossible. By 2:00 A.M., I knew I needed medication, regardless of what risks there might be. I got dressed and walked down the three flights of stairs. On the bottom landing, there were three soldiers surrounded by sandbags with a machine gun pointed toward the front door of the hotel. I carefully stepped around the soldiers, over the sandbags, and made my way to the desk.

The clerk appeared after several coughs and hacks. I told him I needed to see a doctor regardless of martial law. If he could not get one to come to the hotel, I would go to him. He again said it was not possible for anyone to be on the street. No doctor would come out, and I would not be able to get to one. The taxis were not running. A young boy appeared from the office. He was the porter who had taken my suitcase to my room when I checked in. He must have been staying the night in the hotel.

"I will take you to a doctor, Señor," the boy said.

The desk clerk again voiced his objection, but I turned to the boy and said, "Let's go!"

We walked through the darkened streets for about ten minutes, which seemed like an hour. I was having great difficulty breathing and could not stop coughing. I don't think I gave a thought to being shot for breaking curfew. If the porter had any fear, it wasn't apparent.

He took me across a plaza to an ancient-looking building in the darkness. There were no identifying signs. The door was built large enough to allow a horse and carriage to pass in times past. This was one of the many buildings in La Paz that had stood for a hundred years or more with little or no architectural improvements.

The boy hammered on the door as he pushed the doorbell

button. There was no sign that anyone inside had any interest in opening the door. Finally, a crack of light appeared. A Catholic nun in habit appeared and looked suspiciously at us and asked what we wanted in rapidly spoken Spanish. After a short hesitation, she quickly opened and closed the door as we stepped into a large foyer. She led us to a small room with medical equipment.

Ten minutes passed, and a woman doctor appeared, wearing a dressing gown, rubbing sleep from her eyes. She asked a few questions in broken English which I answered to the best of my ability in broken Spanish. She did not need the answers. She said I had a bad case of pneumonia, and she would give me a shot but emphasized that it was necessary that I leave La Paz for a lower altitude as soon as possible. We both knew "as soon as possible" was going to be awhile.

We traced our route back to the hotel. We heard no shots. The patrolling soldiers probably felt comfortable that no one would be foolish enough to venture out during a martial law curfew, and they too slept along with the rest of La Paz. I asked my brave little guide his name. He said "Pepe, señor." I opened my wallet and passed him some currency that made his eyes grow wide. He had a smile that seemed to say the risk was worth it.

Back in my room, I fell into an exhausted sleep hardly knowing when I slept. I had no idea of lapsed time. About noon the next day, Hugo appeared at my door. He brought various over-the-counter medicines and bottles of orange juice. He told me the desk clerk had called him about my illness and he was sorry he couldn't get to me sooner; but soldiers were enforcing the martial law curfew, which had been extended to daylight hours.

Hugo had close friends in high places in government and was able to have a military escort in order to drive to the hotel.

He had a bottle of oxygen which he suggested I use occasionally when short of breath.

Hugo had a plan. As soon as the curfew was lifted and international flights resumed, he would call me. He had made arrangements with Panagra Airlines to call him when they would be allowed to take off for Lima. That way he said I would only be at the 14,000-foot airport for the shortest amount of time.

I stayed in bed for the next two days, mostly in a mental fog and feeling completely miserable. Surely, I survived only due to frequent visits from Hugo bringing medicine, food, and good cheer.

On the fifth day of my visit to La Paz, the curfew was lifted. Hugo's plan went into effect and worked. He drove fast to the airport, passing numerous troops along the way; but we had no interference en route. We drove to the steps of the Boeing 720 Panagra jet. Customs and immigration officials met me at the steps and quickly stamped my passport, and I was finally on my way to Lima.

On arrival at Callao airport in Lima, I was met by Hugo's brother-in-law, who was a Peruvian physician. Hugo had sent a cable ahead for him to meet me. We went quickly to his office and treatment. His final comment to me was, "One more day in La Paz and you would return to Lima in a pine box. You have a bad case of double pneumonia."

I had a couple of weeks in bed in Lima to reflect on my good fortune to have had only five days in La Paz and not six.

Honesty As An Afterthought

This was the third day Gerry Armstrong had a job nailing plywood on windows of abandoned buildings. He was happy to be working after two weeks with nothing to do. Fortunately, it didn't take a lot of skill. He was no carpenter. As long as he measured the window correctly and cut along the penciled lines with the power saw, the plywood sheet would fit. Sometimes it was slightly smaller than it should be, but better that than too long or too wide. He would hammer three out of four nails without bending them. He knew the boss could see the bent nails, but he didn't complain. Gerry would be more careful if he did; he needed the job.

This part of downtown was showing decay. It looked to Gerry like there was lots of work ahead just boarding up windows. Some blocks still had open businesses, but it seemed like the customers were few and far between.

As the work-day ended, Gerry walked to his car parked in the alley, rubbing his sore arm muscles. He was thankful the day was over. As he put his hammer and power saw into the trunk of his beat-up Chevy Nova, Mr. Ortiz, the boss, walked up to him. "Gerry, don't show up for work tomorrow. I don't need you. Here's three days' pay." He handed Gerry an envelope and walked away without another word. Gerry swallowed hard and looked at the back of Ortiz as he got into his shiny new red Ford pickup truck.

Gerry felt very dejected. Tomorrow morning he would have to go to the vacant lot on 22nd Street and join the daily informal worker pool, consisting of drunks with hangovers, vagrants, illegals, and just plain "down and outs" like him. He knew he might be there all day and not get picked up for a job. That was usually the case. He may even have to stoop to taking a day job cutting grass with one of the lawn-care outfits. That would not be his first choice but might be his only choice. For one thing, the pay wasn't worth it--work hard all day for $20 or $30.

Gerry slammed the trunk lid down with a curse. He turned to get in and drive away when he heard the screech of tires. Looking down the street he could see a late-model car coming very fast; close behind was a police car with siren blaring and red and blue lights flashing on top. As the speeding late-model car passed Gerry, a bundle came flying out of the passenger-side window toward him. When the bundle hit the gutter, it burst and spilled the contents onto the sidewalk and into the gutter. It looked like a Safeway plastic grocery bag. Gerry looked at the scattered debris. It consisted of currency and jewelry. He was too dumbfounded to pick anything up. A second police car came speeding up and screeched to a stop in front of Gerry. The first car had been stopped by pursuing police a block down the street. The police had two men out of the car, standing bent over with their hands on the side of the car. He could see the police had handguns pointed at the two men.

Two policemen in front of Gerry began to pick up the scattered money and jewels, putting them in a cloth sack. A group of people, seemingly from out of nowhere, gathered around. Only minutes before, there was no one to be seen; now there were 8 or 10 people staring down at the money and jewels while the police carefully gathered the items. No one else attempted to pick anything up. A medium-sized, mangy, black dog with one white paw, ribs showing, and no collar appeared unnoticed from the alley along the deserted building and joined the onlookers.

As the police picked up the last of the currency, watches, rings, loose stones, and earrings, one of the onlookers, a well-dressed elderly lady, shouted, "Look, the dog has a stone in his mouth! It's an emerald! Stop him!"

The entire crowd and the two policemen surrounded the startled dog. Everyone shouted commands at the bewildered animal. The dog had enough, broke through the forest of legs surrounding him, and ran back down the alley. The entire crowd ran after the dog: the well-dressed lady, the policemen, two teen-age boys, a man in a business suit carrying a brief case, and a young woman in a dress and high heels. The heel of the young woman's left shoe broke, but she continued the pursuit, limping and skipping to keep up with the others, her dress gathered halfway up her thighs.

Gerry didn't join the shouting mob chasing the mongrel. Instead, he got in his car and drove slowly down the street in the opposite direction. Out of sight, he put his hand in his pocket and felt the smooth cold surface of the emerald. With all the shouting, no one noticed the dog had dropped the emerald as he made his getaway. Gerry did. He thought aloud, "They'll have a fat chance catching that dog. No one will ever know what happened to the emerald."

Gerry reached the rooming house still full of excitement. After he parked his rickety and rusty car behind the house, he walked around to the front door and opened it. Inside, Mrs. Bird was standing in the entryway.

"Mr. Armstrong, the rent was due yesterday. You know

the rules. Pay your rent on time, you stay; miss it by one day, and you're out of here!" She had a cigarette dangling from her lips with ashes about to drop. There was a strong smell of cheap wine on her breath which Gerry could detect even at his distance.

Gerry smiled, "Mrs. Bird, you know I always pay my rent. I have the money right here." He opened the pay envelope and took out $280. He counted out $250 and handed the bills to Mrs. Bird. She took the money without a "thank you," put the bills in her robe pocket, turned, and walked to the kitchen. Gerry grimaced and shook his head as she shut the kitchen door behind her.

He walked up the stairs to his room, closed the door, and locked it. He went to the only chair in the bedroom and sat down with the emerald in the palm of his hand. This was the first chance he had to get a good look at the stone. "Beautiful," he said out loud as he turned it over in his hand, feeling the smooth-faceted surfaces. He held it to the light and was surprised by its deep green color and radiance. He wouldn't really have known what kind of gem it was if the elderly lady hadn't said it was an emerald. He guessed the oblong stone was more than an inch long and maybe a half inch wide.

As he turned the emerald over in his hand, he began to realize what he had done. "I didn't really steal it. I found it. Well, yes," he mumbled, "maybe it was stealing, I should have turned it over to the police. But they were chasing the dog. They weren't there when I found it, were they? Not my fault." But that line of thinking was not working. He knew he was wrong. He had never stolen a thing in his life, no matter how desperate he was; and there had been times when he really had been desperate with opportunities to steal, but it never entered his head to take something that didn't belong to him. Never. He was beginning to feel a little sick. He thought he should walk down to Jimmy's Diner. A hamburger might be just what he needed.

At Jimmy's Diner, with the emerald still safely in his pants pocket, he ordered the evening special as described on a chalkboard at the entrance to the diner--a meatloaf dinner instead of a hamburger. That might help his disposition and his stomach even more.

Jimmy Boyles served the special to Gerry, who was sitting at the counter. "You look deep in thought, Gerry," he said, putting a plate of meatloaf and mashed potatoes down. "Whatcha thinkin' about?"

Gerry didn't look up at Jimmy as he replied: "Oh, not much. I lost my job today. I only worked three days. I'll get something to do tomorrow. Hell, I only worked three days in the past two weeks. It's getting pretty desperate out there, Jimmy. I'm pretty near broke. I got $280 today, and only thirty of it is left after I paid rent to that old witch, Mrs. Bird. You know, I don't think she owns a dress. She's always in a ratty, old robe."

Jimmy Boyles wiped his hands on his almost-white apron, gave a sympathetic sigh, shook his head, and went back to the kitchen. Gerry ate in silence. The only sound in the diner, above the clinking of silverware being washed in the kitchen, was the TV hung on metal brackets high in the corner. The local news was on, and an announcer was describing the day's big story--the Albert Stein's Jewelry Store robbery.

Gerry stopped eating abruptly, put his fork on the plate, and stopped chewing on the tough meatloaf special. The announcer had a forced smile on his face as he opened the newscast with, "A jewelry store robbery today: Police have two suspects in custody, as well as the stolen items. The robbery occurred at 4:40 this afternoon. Two suspects reportedly walked into the Albert Stein Jewelry Store on Main Street and, at gunpoint, demanded cash and jewelry be put into a plastic bag they handed a salesclerk. During the robbery, a store employee set off a silent alarm which summoned police who arrived within minutes, interrupting the robbery. The suspects fled in a late-model car. The car had been reported stolen earlier.

"As police pursued the vehicle, the suspects threw the plastic bag out of the car at 1800 Peach Avenue. Police recovered the items shortly thereafter. There were no injuries. The recovered goods will be returned to the Albert Stein Jewelry Store when investigations have been completed.

"Mr. Stein, owner of the store, has reported that a highly valuable emerald reportedly was taken by a stray dog. The dog has not yet been traced. Police advise they will continue to search for the dog; however, a police spokesman stated there is little hope that either the emerald or the dog will be found. In other news...."

Gerry turned his attention back to the meatloaf but lost interest in finishing it. He called Jimmy to bring the check. Jimmy put the check on the counter in front of Gerry and looked at the half-eaten meal. "What's the matter; you don't like my cookin? You must be sicker than you look."

"No, your cooking is fine. I just don't have an appetite right now; got a lot of things on my mind." He put the exact amount of change on the counter, turned, and walked out of the diner, calling over his shoulder, "Thanks, Jimmy, see you later."

Gerry returned to the rooming house and went directly to his room. He sat on the edge of the bed. What to do now. He felt covered by a blanket of guilt. Too late to go to the police, he might be arrested. The way he was dressed, they might even arrest him on vagrancy charges. He couldn't take the emerald to the jewelry store; they would surely call the police, and he would be back at square one. There was one thing he could do. He wasn't happy with the idea, but maybe it was the only option.

Two years before, when he left Houston, he had pawned his guitar, watch, radio, camera, and suitcase just to get enough money to move to Denver.

He would drive back to Houston, go to the same pawn shop, and pawn the emerald. Houston was far enough away; nobody there would know about the missing emerald. Besides, they weren't looking for a thief; they were looking for a black mongrel dog with one white paw. "That's the plan," he mused.

He went to the closet and pulled a small wooden box from under his socks and a folded sweatshirt. Inside the box was all the money he had. He counted out the currency and change--a total of $175.89. Adding the money he had left from the three days' pay, made a total of $192.89. That was all he had between there and a park bench; but it should be enough to get to Houston, providing he didn't have car trouble or a blowout. He would also be sleeping in his car and eating very little until he cashed in on the emerald. It was a big gamble but he saw no other way.

As Gerry entered the outskirts of Houston, he felt very comfortable that everything was going as planned. It was getting late in the afternoon, and he would never be able to get to the pawn shop on Fannin Street before it closed. He did not want to sleep in the car in Houston. The police probably would find him and make him move on no matter where he parked. Above all, he didn't want to be searched, which they would likely do, looking for drugs and even stolen goods. He would never be able to explain the emerald in his pocket. Big trouble. He pulled into a Motel 6. He didn't like the idea of spending money for a room, but it was the safest thing to do--even if there wasn't much left.

The next morning, he checked out of the motel and drove directly to the Texas Rebel Pawn Shop on Fannin Street. He was hungry but pushed the thought from his mind, concentrating on the story he would tell the pawnbroker. The shop was open. He went in and looked around. He was the only customer. The pawnbroker was behind the counter and didn't bother to look up at Gerry as he approached the counter.

"What can I do for you son?"Gerry didn't think it was the same man who had handled his pawned items previously. That was good.

"I have an emerald that was left to me by a great aunt when she passed away last month. I'm a little short of cash and would like to pawn it. I don't know how much it's worth. This is it." Gerry took the gem from his pocket and placed it on the glass countertop.

The pawnbroker gave Gerry a long, suspicious look, took the emerald, looked at it briefly with his jeweler's glass, put it back on the counter, and said, "Well, son, it's not a real emerald but a pretty good synthetic imitation. Maybe it could be used in costume jewelry."

Gerry could not hide his disappointment. He had gone through so much trouble to get to this point. The emerald, or whatever it was, was a curse. "How much will you give me for it?" He asked the pawnbroker, not trying to conceal his hurt.

The broker was back at his writing, not bothering to look up: "Twenty dollars; take it or leave it."

Gerry was silent for a few thoughtful moments and replied, "O.K., I'll take it."

The broker, took a pawn receipt book from a desk behind the counter, wrote out the receipt and asked for Gerry's name and address. "Bob White," Gerry replied and gave a made-up Houston address. The broker passed the pawn ticket to Gerry with a twenty-dollar bill and took the stone from the counter, opened a sliding glass door, and put the stone on a shelf along with assorted silver jewelry, dusty watches, and other pawns with tags attached.

Gerry put the twenty dollars in his pocket and walked out of the pawnshop. He got in his car and headed for the interstate. He knew he had to get back to Denver and get a job of some sort. He hoped he would have enough money to buy gas to make it back. The whole effort had been a stupid idea.

The pawnbroker watched Gerry leave the store. When he was satisfied he was gone, he reached in and took the emerald from the glass pawn case and smiled. He walked to the old steel safe in the corner of the shop, pulled open the heavy door, carefully put the emerald on a shelf, shut the door, and rubbed his hands together with a wide, satisfied grin.

Gerry had covered almost ten miles along the interstate, feeling very dejected. He had acted wrongly and knew it. At the next exit, he left the interstate, looped back onto the highway, and returned to Houston. He drove to the pawnshop, parked the car, and went in. There was a look of surprise--almost shock--on the broker's face.

"I've changed my mind; I'd like to redeem my pawn. Here's the ticket." Gerry noticed there were two people in the shop looking at pawns in the glass case, a policeman and another man in a suit. The broker glanced at them as well.

The broker spoke quietly: "What? You want me to give you your pawn back? Are you sure? Why did you bring it to me in the first place if you didn't want to pawn it?" He glanced again at the two men. He certainly didn't want a scene with them in the store. Gerry put the twenty-dollar bill on the counter.

"I'll have to charge you ten dollars. You sure you want it now? Why not think about it awhile? I'll always be here."

"No. I don't want to think about it. I want it. Take your ten dollars and give it to me." Gerry was getting impatient, raising his voice. He wanted the emerald back before he changed his mind.

The pawnbroker walked to the safe, took the emerald out, and handed it to Gerry with obvious disgust. Gerry took the stone, put it in his pocket, and handed the pawnbroker the twenty plus a ten-dollar bill from his wallet, and walked out, glancing once more at the two men who were also looking at him as he closed the pawnshop door. He got in the car and retraced the route to the interstate.

Back in Denver, hungry, tired, and with two days' beard growth, he had made up his mind. He drove directly to the Albert Stein Jewelry Store, parked in the lot, and walked into the elegant shop. A salesclerk asked if she could help him.

"I'd like to talk to Mr. Stein."

The salesclerk narrowed her eyes and said a little sarcastically, "May I ask why you would like to speak to Mr. Stein?"

"It's personal," he replied.

The clerk gave a shrug and, with disdain, dialed Stein's extension. "There's a gentleman to see you, sir." She hung up the phone; turned to Gerry and said: "Mr. Stein will be with you in a moment." The clerk moved away to greet a couple, who were entering the store.

"I'm Albert Stein; what can I do for you, son?" Stein gave

Gerry a long look, taking in his unshaven face and rumpled clothes.

"Mr. Stein, I believe this is yours." He took the emerald from his pocket and handed it to Stein.

Stein looked shocked. "Good lord! I don't believe it! How can I ever thank you? I had no hope of ever seeing this emerald again. You wouldn't believe how valuable it is! You are a very, very honest person, young man. Come into my office."

Stein led the way. The counter clerks in the store looked on with question. What had made Mr. Stein so happy?

"Please sit down. What's your name? Where did you find the emerald? How did you know it belonged to me?" Stein was all smiles. He took a large checkbook from a drawer in his polished desk and began writing a check. Gerry casually explained how he found the emerald in an alley near a place where he used to work and gave his real name and real address. He said he remembered the theft report on the TV news and the story about the missing emerald.

Stein handed the check to Gerry. Gerry took a deep breath, as he looked at the amount--five hundred dollars! He found it difficult to focus on the check. His hand began to shake. Stein broke the silence with a serious tone, "Mr. Armstrong, I would like you to consider coming to work for me. If you are agreeable, I will run all the necessary background checks. I have a courier position open which I haven't been able to fill. You have proved your honesty without question." Gerry hardly heard anything from, "I would like you to consider coming to work for me."

Gerry walked out of the Albert Stein Jewelry Store in a daze. He looked at the $500 check over and over as he strolled to the parking lot and got into his car.

Back at the rooming house, Gerry emptied the small closet and dresser drawers, put his clothes in a small cardboard box, walked down the stairs, and called to Mrs. Bird.

"Mrs. Bird, I'm moving out. Keep the advance rent. Good-bye." As he opened the door to leave, he said, "I'll let you know my new address in case I get any mail."

Mrs. Bird stood in the kitchen doorway, dressed in her usual bathrobe, cigarette dangling from her pursed lips. "You might have given me some notice. I hope you didn't leave the room in a mess." She turned her back on Gerry and walked into the kitchen.

Gerry drove to Jimmy's Diner. He sat at his usual stool at the counter. Jimmy poked his head through the serving hatch. "Hey, Gerry, where you been? Haven't seen you for nearly a week."

"Well, Jimmy, a lot has happened since I last saw you. I took a quick trip back to Houston. Went to visit an old great aunt," he said, turning his eyes away from Jimmy. "Remember that robbery at the Albert Stein Jewelry Store? I found the emerald the dog ran off with." He spoke quickly, hoping Jimmy wouldn't ask questions about when or where he found the gem. "Today, I took it to the jewelry store and gave it to Stein. He was so happy to get it back, he gave me a $500 reward!" Gerry took the folded check from his pocket and held it up for Jimmy to see.

"Wow! You're one lucky guy, Gerry. I guess honesty really does pay, huh?" Jimmy came out of the kitchen carrying a mug of coffee and put it on the lunch counter in front of Gerry. "On the house. Whatcha gonna do with all that money?"

"First of all, I have to find another place to room. I moved out of that old witch's rooming house. Mr. Stein said he'd give me a job after he did some sort of a background check. So, I'll hang around to see what happens." Gerry took a sip of coffee. "Maybe I'll go back down an' see if Ortiz might need me. Yeah, I think I'll do that." He slid off the counter stool and walked quickly to the cafe's door.

"Hey, Gerry, where an' when did'ya find that emerald?" The questions stopped Gerry before he could get out of the door.

Gerry hesitated a moment, turned, and walked slowly back to the counter stool. He sat down, lowered his head, and said, "Jimmy, I'm gonna level with you. I don't have a great aunt in Houston. I lied to you. I don't know why." He then recounted the details of his week's adventure in dishonesty.

When Gerry finished, Jimmy walked around the counter and sat down on a stool next to him. "Gerry, you are an honest guy; if you weren't, you wouldn't have told me the truth. We'll keep it between us." Trying to add a little levity, Jimmy said, "Hey, I think you owe that dog something. He's the one who deserves the reward!" Jimmy chuckled. Gerry shook his head vigorously.

Gerry smiled: "You know, Jimmy, I always thought I was an honest person. I was wrong." He put a dollar on the counter. "That's for the coffee. I don't want any more conscience problems." He laughed, shook hands, and headed for the door. "Thanks again, Jimmy. I appreciate your understanding. That dog does deserve part of the reward. In a way, he taught me a lesson. See you later." He went to his car and drove away.

Some weeks later, Gerry could be seen driving an emerald green Buick with "Stein Jewelry" discreetly painted on the door; or he could often be seen strolling along in the financial district, in a pin-stripe suit, carrying a shiny, black leather briefcase; at his side was a medium-sized, well-groomed, black dog with one white paw and a jeweled collar.

Sunday Morning Ride

What a joy to drive down the street and wave to the neighbors. Milo turned the corner from Rosedale to St. Ambrose Street. Elm trees made a thick umbrella overhead and shaded the way with occasional thin shafts of bright sunlight. It would be more enjoyable if Milo could continue down Rosedale and beyond, but both parents admonished him to go only around the block and not one block beyond. To violate that rule would surely mean he would no longer be allowed to even go around the block. The privilege would likely be revoked. Milo wouldn't like that to happen, and there were plenty of people in the neighborhood who would happily tell his parents if they saw him. He wouldn't take the chance.

Instead, he would drive slowly and carefully, if only to prove he was responsible; who knows, that might eventually open up more routes for him to explore. Maybe he would even be able to drive to the mountains instead of just "pretending to be riding through the mountains."

As Milo headed down St. Ambrose Street, he could see the Watts' fox terrier, hiding behind a bush in a crouch, ready to bark and attack. He was right. The dog shot out after him yapping as he nipped at the right rear tire. This was no surprise. Every time Milo passed the Watts' house, he expected the same when the dog was out. In fact, he would slow down purposely to see if the dog would chase after the car.

He drove past Mr. and Mrs. Clump, who were always friendly to him. He waved vigorously. Mr. Clump shouted as he passed, "How's the car running, Milo?" Milo shouted back, "Just fine, Mr. Clump." Milo felt proud to have Mr. Clump ask the question which he often did. Mr. Clump was a mechanic, who worked at the Skelly gas station a couple of blocks away on Newberry Street. Milo thought it nice to see Mr. Clump dressed up in a dark blue suit with a bright white shirt and a blue tie, which matched his suit. He was usually in grease-stained overalls. Because it was Sunday morning, the Clumps most likely were on their way to church. Mrs. Clump, always very kind to Milo, sometimes gave him freshly baked cookies when he walked by their house. He liked to visit Mrs. Clump. He thought she could be Santa Claus if she was a man with a white beard. She had snow-white hair and a shape much like Santa's.

Milo rode on. Before he turned to Cherry Street, he passed in front of Buzz Hogan's house on the corner. He didn't like to see Buzz sitting on the steps. He knew he would say something hateful. Buzz shouted, "You're nothing but a little show-off, Milo. Who do you think you are? Some kind of race driver you are. Are you practicing to be in the Indy 500? Ha, ha, ha! That'll be the day. You'll never see it." He turned the corner onto Cherry and ignored Buzz. He was the neighborhood bully. Maybe he was nasty because he was fat and had lots of pimples on his face. Maybe that made him mean.

Milo strained his eyes looking down Cherry Street. He was trying to see if Lois Sweeney was sitting on the front porch. He couldn't see anyone. He went slowly past her house. No one was on the porch. He sped up. He thought, "I'll make another trip around the block. She might be on the swing when I pass by next time." He took in the strong fragrance of the peonies in bloom that lined the Sweeney's sidewalk. The aroma made him a little excited.

He waved to the Rooneys as they pushed a baby carriage along the sidewalk. They lived next door to Milo's house. Mr. Rooney nodded his head; Mrs. Rooney smiled.

He turned the corner slowly and headed up Oak Street and sped up as he passed old Mr. Roach. Mr. Roach didn't even bother to look at Milo, and Milo didn't look at him. Milo thought Mr. Roach was just an old grump.

He turned the corner and headed down Rosedale past his house; waved once again at the Clumps, who had crossed to the opposite side of the street; rounded the corner to St. Ambrose Street; and then sped fast enough that the fox terrier didn't bother to chase him. He passed Buzz Hogan's house. Thank goodness, Buzz wasn't sitting out in front this time. He rounded the corner at Cherry Street.

Again, he looked at the Sweeney's house. This time she was there sitting on the porch swing! He slowed down, hoping she hadn't seen him coming--at least not yet. She was beautiful. He thought she looked like an angel in her bright, white Sunday dress with her golden hair draped over her shoulders. She looked like the angels in the stained-glass windows at the church. As he approached the Sweeney's house, he accelerated a little more and was careful not to look at Lois but hoped she was watching him. His heart beat a little faster. Milo quickly turned the corner. He saw Mr. Roach standing on the corner trying to cross the street, and once again they ignored one another. By the time he reached his house, Lois was forgotten. He stopped in front of his house. His father was sitting on the porch.

"Milo," his father called, "I hear a loud squeaky noise. I think I'll have to oil those pedals on your kiddie car."

The English Oak Rocking Chair

Cold winds seeped through gaps in the croft door and mixed with the peat-fire smoke escaping around the hearth. Occasional rain showers added dampness to the room. Laird Wallace rubbed his arms to lessen the chill. He put a wood chisel on the work bench, took a woolen sweater from the coat hook on back of the door, pulled it over his head, and felt the weight heavy on his shoulders. He didn't like to work in the sweater, it was very restrictive and hampered his arm when he tried to do delicate work. Nonetheless, he needed the warmth. The damp cold irritated his side. As if to be sure the musket ball was still lodged above his hip, he felt the hard lump. Yes, it's still there he mused, knowing that it would always be there--right to the grave. As part of the ritual, he cursed the "Frenchie" who put it there; at least he blamed a "Frenchie" but knew it might have been a shot from friendly troops, even from one of his comrades.

On that terrible day, the 18th June, 1815, fighting was fierce; shots were fired at random without aim and in fear without concern for where the musket ball would land or hit. Men were falling everywhere he looked, some without a murmur and some with screams that could be heard above the constant, loud noise of battle.

He bent over his work table and stared into the wood shavings thinking that he must stop remembering. He would not ever return to the carefree life he lived before being recruited by the Highland Light Infantry and before being sent to Belgium to meet the feared Army of Napoleon, where he would live or die on the rolling farm fields of Waterloo. He knew when he was struck by the musket ball early in the battle that he, too, must have screamed as loudly as any of the others when he fell to the churned-up ground, then to be stepped on by comrades with bayonets flashing, rushing to meet French soldiers as they rushed to meet British soldiers, also stepping on-or-over their fallen comrades. Later, he recognized his good fortune to be a casualty early in the day and to be on the winning side as well. But that good fortune did not wipe away the horror of the day, nor the pain of the musket ball, not even these ten years later.

Laird pushed the painful thoughts from his mind and again was carefully, almost gently, shaping pieces of English oak. He had already spent much more time with this piece of furniture than any other he had made; and over the years, he had made hundreds of pieces of the highest-quality furniture. His finely made furniture had been ordered by some of the richest land owners in the area. His reputation as a fine craftsman was known beyond the county. Spending so much of his workday on this one piece would reduce his income, but it didn't matter. He would put his best workmanship into this particular piece of furniture; and it would never be sold, at least not by him. It would be his--his personal rocking chair. This rocking chair would be built to last for as long as any piece of furniture could last and it would have more than just superior workmanship. This rocking chair would have a soul, shaped from aged English Oak with his feelings put into every cut and scrape, every coat of stain, and every coat of polish. As an artist strives to paint a masterpiece in oil or watercolors, or a sculptor chips away at granite to make a statue of unequaled beauty, Laird had but one thought and one effort--to make the most beautiful English Oak rocking chair that had ever been crafted, or ever would be crafted for that matter.

Weeks later, the prize was finished. He placed it near the hearth; and when he wasn't busy at his workbench, he was in the rocking chair. He could feel the shape of the back and the comfort of the seat just as he designed it. He was always pleased with his craftsmanship whenever he sat in it. All joints fit with such precision that only a thin hairline could be seen. Even the grain was closely matched to give the impression that the oak actually grew into a rocking chair.

When customers appeared at his croft, all would marvel at the workmanship of the rocking chair; and many would make an effort to buy it to no avail.

After years of excellent furniture creation, Laird Wallace realized the rewards of hard, careful work. He had expanded his furniture-making enterprise several times until he had a staff of expert furniture makers working for him. As age took its toll on his body and arthritis prevented his hands from moving as he wished, he became an observer of his furniture-making operation, constantly advising and suggesting techniques to his employees until each piece of furniture was finished as though he had made it himself. He had long before moved from his meager confines of the croft and built a stately brick home overlooking the tranquil valley and the old vine-covered croft.

In the fall of 1877, Laird sat contentedly in his treasured rocking chair, his hand holding the hard lump that surrounded the musket ball. He rocked gently until the rocking chair slowed to a stop. Only Laird's head dropped, his chin on his chest. The fine old rocker held his body from falling, unwilling to release its creator.

The auction drew buyers from Scotland, England, and

even France. Laird Wallace's reputation as a fine furniture fabricator was known to royalty, the wealthy, and any dealer who appreciated the value of excellently made furniture. Laird had sold his furniture throughout the British Isles, but some specially made pieces of a new design or extra-fine craftsmanship would occasionally end up in his manor house. Everything was to be sold, including his precious rocking chair. The rocking chair was considered to be the most valuable of the pieces and was auctioned last. Heavy bidding was finally reduced to three serious buyers. The representative of the Burton family of Cardiff was rewarded for his bidding persistence--and money.

The Burton estate was well-known in the Cardiff area. The wealth was built over a century from wool production. True, Dai Burton inherited not only the estate from his father, who had inherited it from his father, but each in their turn contributed to the sizable fortune through accumulation of money and acquisition of land.

With each war fought by the British Empire, beginning with the revolution in the American colonies, Burton wealth increased greatly. Burton wool was woven into the uniforms worn by British troops as they marched to battle on every continent, at one time or another. The torn and bloody woolen uniforms were also buried on every continent.

From birth, Dai Burton enjoyed the finer things of life and developed a special appreciation for fine furniture. He was proud of his furniture collection and would often mention the value. Over the years, he had learned of the beautiful furniture produced by one Laird Wallace of Scotland; and at news of Wallace's death and an estate auction, he sent his most-trusted furniture dealer to attend with instructions to buy the best piece at any price.

He was not disappointed. The Wallace rocking chair was

surely the most unusual, most-perfect piece of crafted furniture he had ever seen and became the signature piece of his collection. Moreover, he used it, and it became an escape for him. As he slowly rocked, it was a means for his mind to escape from business and family concerns. He felt secure whenever he sat in the rocking chair. His secret, never revealed, was simply that he felt he was a very young child once again and on his mother's lap. He would smile slightly at the image whenever he was in the rocker. His concerns would actually seem to be less as he rocked.

In the year of 1880, a third daughter was born to Mrs. Burton. She was named Victoria, with the queen in mind at the christening. From the age of two weeks, Dai Burton rocked his daughter in his precious rocking chair. He hadn't rocked the other children as babies, but now he believed the beautiful English oak rocking chair was made especially to rock a baby to sleep. Of course, this unusual activity was kept very private. The servants were not to know, nor the other children. It was not a usual performance by a country squire. Only Mrs. Burton was aware, and she certainly would not mention to a soul Dai Burton's rocking the baby, Victoria.

During the early years, Dai Burton and Victoria became very close. As Victoria grew older and began talking in sentences, the rocking chair became their secret meeting place. She would tell her father her deepest thoughts, her fears, and above all, her expectations. Burton would also confide his thoughts to Victoria; she would listen dutifully as he rocked. Not understanding, she would drift off to a peaceful sleep. Dai Burton and Victoria became as close as a parent and child could be.

The year 1911 was a special time for the Burton family. Victoria had her first child. Although Dai Burton did not fully approve of Victoria's marriage to Dudley Jones the previous year, believing he was not a suitable husband for his Victoria, he admitted to himself, there was no suitable husband for Victoria. He also had to admit to himself that Jones was a very competent solicitor. He had gained an enviable reputation very early in his practice and was sought after by notable businessmen, as well as some royalty.

When Victoria broke the news to the family that Dudley had decided to move to America, it was a shock for Burton. He tried desperately to convince Jones to change his plans, but Victoria emotionally sided with Dudley favoring his plan. Burton could see he was losing the battle. Not money, nor offers of gifts of property, nor friendly chats with brandy after dinners had any impact on Jones or Victoria for that matter. So plans were made and passage for the three Jones' was booked on the newly built luxury liner called the "Titanic."

Burton wept openly as he told Victoria he was giving her his prized rocking chair as a parting gift. Deep in his thoughts, he couldn't bear to think what would happen to the rocking chair upon his death. He knew Victoria held the rocker in much the same esteem as he had over the years. Although, it was more than eighty years old, it had the appearance of having just been crafted. The finish was without a mar of any sort. When he spoke to Victoria about the gift, she protested and also wept. He arranged for their selected household furnishings, including the rocking chair, to be shipped ahead to assure the furnishings would be there on their arrival in America at their final destination. He suggested it would be one less concern for Dudley as he took up his new appointment at a brewery in Potosi, Wisconsin.

Burton died of a heart attack three days after hearing the tragic news of the Titanic disaster. From the moment he was notified, he fell into a deep depression and spoke to no one. His grief was unbearable.

In the early 1900s, Potosi, Wisconsin was struggling to

become something of a real town. It never succeeded. The brewery was the main business in town; and aside from farm work, provided the only real employment for the sparse inhabitants. The Burton household shipment had arrived in good shape and was stored in the brewery.

Six months after the Titanic disaster, Charlie Schmidt, general manager of the brewery, received a letter from Mrs. Burton authorizing the brewery to sell the Jones' belongings and remit the proceeds to her in Cardiff. Schmidt had doubts that anyone in the Potosi area would have an interest in buying much of the Jones' household goods. He advertised in the county newspaper, set a date for the sale, and hoped someone would buy the lot. He needed the warehouse space and didn't want to store bits and pieces if everything was not sold. On the day of the sale, a dozen or so curious townspeople and farmers from the area gathered in the warehouse. The sale created some local interest because Schmidt had advertised that the goods had belonged to a family from Wales who were lost in the sinking of the Titanic. Nevertheless, there was only one serious buyer, a used-furniture dealer from Milwaukee, who offered to buy the entire container for a lump-sum price. Schmidt was delighted. He was not concerned with the very low price that was offered. He collected the money and arranged for a transfer to Mrs. Burton in Wales, as directed.

Over the next few years, the used-furniture dealer sold the various furniture pieces and household goods from his Milwaukee warehouse. The English oak rocking chair was displayed in a warehouse window bordering the street. It had accumulated a gray cover of dust. Cobwebs were like lacework between the rungs. The rocker's fine finish wasn't visible under the shroud of dust.

Peter Pelts walked slowly down Milwaukee Avenue and turned down a side street. He was just killing time until the

3:03 P.M. train for Chicago. He had been in Milwaukee for a week and had purchased new equipment for the lumbermill back in Silver City. In Chicago, he would board the Santa Fe for Albuquerque. He stopped to look in the furniture warehouse window. His eye caught the English Oak rocking chair. He had worked with wood all his career and immediately recognized the craftsmanship put into the rocker.

"What a fine piece of furniture," he thought to himself. "Bettie would really appreciate that rocker." Although Bettie was just 10 years old, she had become very responsible and very adult since the death of Mrs. Pelts. She had been without her mother's love and care for nearly two years, and Peter knew he was no substitute for his wife. "I will get that rocking chair for her-- a gift from my trip." He thought for a moment that perhaps a doll with a porcelain head would be a more suitable gift, but he had waited too long to go shopping. There wasn't much time left before the 3:03 would board. He went into the store; a bell attached to the top of the door announced his entry. The used-furniture dealer greeted him. "What can I do for you, sir?"

"How much is that rocking chair in the window?" Peter pointed to the dust-covered rocker.

The furniture dealer went to the rocker and blew dust from the seat. "This is a fine piece of furniture. It is quite expensive. But, I have had it for a good while and need the space. I'll reduce the price if you will take it now." He quoted a price. Peter thought it too high and offered a lower price. The used-furniture dealer frowned and said he accepted. Peter asked that it be wrapped in newspaper as he had to take it on a train all the way to Albuquerque.

At the Milwaukee Railroad Depot, Peter checked the rocking chair at the freight window, asking the attendant to be particularly careful. He didn't want it damaged. The attendant looked up through his green visor shade and said he would do his best. He would put a fragile tag on the chair but couldn't guarantee what would happen when it got to Union Station in Chicago. "Those people down there are real roughnecks. They don't treat anything too gently. I get lots of complaints."

The attendant finished the paperwork and picked the rocker up to put it on the dock. "This thing must be made of iron! It's really heavy. How did you manage to carry it in here alone?" He looked at Peter. Peter shrugged and agreed it was heavy. When the dust was wiped from the rocker and he sat in it in the used-furniture warehouse, he knew he had to have it. It was such a beautiful piece of workmanship that he experienced a warm feeling when he sat in it. It was more than just comfortable. He couldn't think why the rocker gave him such an unusual sensation. He hoped Bettie would have the same experience and appreciation.

The journey back to New Mexico was long and tiring. Peter took every opportunity to inspect his treasured rocking chair which was stored in the freight compartment of the train. He made sure it was handled with care at each transfer. When he arrived at the Hurley, New Mexico, station, he arranged for a freight hauler to transport the rocker over the rough dirt road to his home north of Silver City near Pinos Altos.

The entire effort was worth it. Bettie was overjoyed with the rocking chair. Peter carefully undid the protective newspaper covering. There was no damage. When Bettie saw the rocker, she screamed with delight. She immediately got in the chair and rocked for several minutes until Peter had to say, "That's enough rocking, Bettie."   He laughed. "Surely, you will wear that rocking chair out!"

Bettie stopped rocking but remained in the chair. She became quiet and serene. Peter suspected she was having the same experience he had had when he first sat in the rocking chair. She rubbed her hand over the rocking chair arms and felt the satin finish. She turned her head toward her father and said, "Thank you. This is the most beautiful present I have ever gotten. Thank you." She jumped from the rocker and embraced her father tightly around his waist.

Bettie married Ralph Ward. She had known him from grade-school days. They were well suited for one another. Ralph began working in the sawmill for Bettie's father when he was 16 years old. He hadn't finished high school. Bettie and Ralph were barely 21 years old when they were married. Their firstborn was named Peter after Bettie's father. He was rocked in Bettie's rocking chair from his second day on earth. Bettie had lovingly kept the rocker in the same pristine condition from the day she watched her father unwrap it. She had spent many hours rocking in the old English Oak rocking chair. All through her youth and into adulthood, she spent hours in the rocking chair reading novels and classical literature, doing homework, knitting, and tatting. Bettie often found comfort and solace just sitting in the rocker, seemingly doing nothing.

After Peter was born she spent even more time in her rocking chair, so much time that Ralph would often comment that if she didn't get out of that old rocking chair, she would die in it. He could not have known how prophetic the remark would be.

In 1945, the family received a cable which read, "The President of the United States and the Secretary of War regret to inform you that your son, Corporal Peter Ward was killed in action while trying to rescue a wounded comrade during a battle with the Japanese in the South Pacific. He has been awarded the Silver Star for bravery beyond the call of duty...."

Bettie spent most of the days and weeks to follow, rocking in the old English Oak rocker. A short time later, Ralph returned home from the sawmill and found Bettie sitting lifeless in the old rocker, head on her chest. The rocking chair seemed to hold her, keeping her from falling to the floor.

Ralph no longer wanted to see the rocking chair in the house. A few weeks after the funeral, he offered it to one of the temporary sawmill employees, if he would come and pick it up.

In a hippy commune in northern New Mexico, a sixteen-year old girl sat in the rocking chair in the cluttered living room of a makeshift log cabin with a corrugated tin roof. The old English Oak rocking chair was painted pink on one arm, garish green on the other, a deep shade of purple on the back, and now had red and orange rockers. The young girl complained loudly to Jake, her twenty-two-year-old, live-in boyfriend, that the rocking chair was uncomfortable and they should sell it. They would get a little money from it to buy some pot. Jake agreed.

In a village in the Colorado mountains, the gaudily painted rocking chair sat on a covered porch in front of a second-hand store. Amos Collier was a volunteer working with a newly built retirement home. He had agreed to find inexpensive furnishings for the lobby. As he drove his pickup past the second-hand store, the rocking chair caught his attention. He stopped and got a closer look. The old folks would appreciate a rocker, he thought, but not with those colors. He offered to buy the rocking chair while holding a few dollar bills in his hand. The owner didn't refuse the offer. He put the chair in the back of his truck and drove home.

In his garage workshop, Amos began to remove the garish paint. As the underlying wood became exposed, he realized that he was working with no ordinary rocking chair. Then, over days, he carefully restored the finish, removed scratches, and repaired marks and blemishes, no matter how small. When he finished, he felt the wood must be close to the original condition. He looked at the superior workmanship and couldn't help wondering who had made such a magnificent piece of furniture. He believed it to be old and possibly from Europe. He couldn't imagine much beyond those thoughts.

There was genuine appreciation when the rocking chair was delivered to the retirement home. The residents took turns sitting in the chair and some had to be told to give others a chance to try the rocker.

That rocking chair still sits in the retirement-home lobby. It is cared for as well as any previous owner had cared for it. It is lovingly kept polished and dusted. Children of all ages often sit and rock, usually with a serene smile. Over the years, many residents have sat for hours at a time in the rocker; some were found later with their chins on their chests, still sitting upright, mysteriously held by the rocking chair.

You may ask: "How do I know these things?" I will tell you how I know. "I *am* that old English Oak rocking chair--lovingly made with a soul."